Miriam March 14 '2017

Six Days in June

The Havenport Murders

SIX DAYS IN JUNE

The Havenport Murders

THE SECOND HARRISON HUNT MYSTERY

PAUL EISEMAN

AuthorHouse™ LLC
1663 Liberty Drive
Bloomington, IN 47403
www.authorhouse.com
Phone: 1-800-839-8640

Published by AuthorHouse 09/12/2013

ISBN: 978-1-4918-1353-9 (sc)
ISBN: 978-1-4918-1352-2 (hc)
ISBN: 978-1-4918-1336-2 (e)

Library of Congress Control Number: 2013916107

For: Phyllis and Ben
and Fred

Chapter 1

As usual, Sophie was right. I did need a rest. Badly. And after a year like the last one, who wouldn't? Actually, it had been thirteen months. Thirteen tumultuous, exhilarating, unbelievably exciting but exhausting months. It had been on the Wednesday afternoon of May 14th of last year that I had solved the Brookfield murders. The amount of attention I then received from the media was unprecedented. After all, it was not every day that a New York City theatrical director and playwright, however talented he might be, was lauded as "A Sherlock Holmes for the 21st century" (*Newsweek*), "Super-sleuth director Harrison Hunt" (*USA Today*), and "A Master of Ratiocination Proves Himself a True Renaissance Man" (*The New York Review of Books*), my favorites among many, many others.

The third panegyric quoted above headlined that publication's review of my book. Oh yes, I had written a book. After my Oprah interview, I was inundated with offers from publishers to write the definitive details of the events in Brookfield. Titled *Five Days in May*, it reached number four on the New York Times' nonfiction bestseller list and is obtainable at your local neighborhood bookstore. (If any of this sadly dying breed can still be found.) After the book was published, I became a darling (and highly compensated) member of the lecture circuit. The dictation of the book to Sophie, the book signing tour, the sold out lectures all had to be spaced around the rehearsals for the Broadway production of the plays I had workshopped in Brookfield. They opened to acclaim and four Tony nominations. So it had indeed been a whirlwind thirteen months, and Sophie was undeniably correct. I did need a rest and a long one.

Hence it certainly seemed fortuitous when Sophie received the phone call a month or so ago from Madge Magill. Sophie and Madge had become good friends when they were both employed at Yale Drama School. Sophie had worked in the dean's office and Madge in the school's library. I had met Sophie when I was a student there, and the two of us had immediately hit it off. After I graduated and learned that Sophie had left Yale, I asked her to assist me on a production I was directing in the city. That was well over twenty years ago, and our working relationship had continued and our friendship had grown from then on. Madge had remained at Yale Drama and had eventually been promoted to the position of head librarian and keeper of the school's archives. In that capacity, she had provided valuable information that helped solve the Brookfield murders.

When Madge had attended the opening night celebration of my two new plays in Brookfield last July, she told Sophie that she planned to retire in a year's time and permanently move to the remote fishing village of Havenport. Madge's family had owned a spacious home there for generations, and she had enjoyed spending time there every summer since she was a child. After her parents had died a decade or so ago, she had inherited the house and property and had yearned to live year-round in that tiny community on the rocky New England coast she loved so much.

The reason she had delayed leaving New Haven was her son Edward's education. One of the perks Madge enjoyed as an employee of the university was substantially reduced tuition for immediate family members. Now that Edward was graduating with honors from Yale College, Madge was finally free to fulfill her dream. She had phoned Sophie last month and invited her and "that dear Mr. Hunt" to be the first house guests to celebrate her new move. Sophie had visited Havenport several summers ago and had raved about the scenery, the fresh air and Madge's hospitality. So it didn't take much bullying on Sophie's part for me to agree to accept the generous offer to spend the month of June on the edge of the Atlantic to relax, rejuvenate and recharge my batteries away from the hustle, bustle, glamour and clamor of New York. Sophie and I would return to Manhattan the end of June to attend the Tony awards television broadcast en route to London. We were scheduled to begin the stressful labors of restaging the new plays in the West End in July. Perhaps I might even have the time at Madge's quiet retreat to do more work on the epic tragedy I had begun writing last year.

In a short week's time after accepting Madge's invitation, Sophie and I boarded the Amtrak at Penn Station after posing for a few photographs demanded by those pesky paparazzi and signing soon-to-be treasured autographs for delighted passersby. I withstood these obligations of fame with much more equanimity than did Sophie who had one or two rather ripe remarks for the intrusive photographers. Nevertheless, the train voyage was pleasant as was the subsequent hour-long drive by limousine. The latter had kindly been arranged by Madge. We arrived in the village greeted by the most brilliant sunset I had ever experienced. The rose-colored rays bathed the exteriors of the old weathered houses we passed with impressionistic pastels, and the welcoming tones of Madge's door chimes complemented somehow the roar of the waves crashing on the rocks below her charming 1840's shingled colonial. I was in Havenport, and I loved it.

I loved the ever changing views of the ocean especially when seen from the balcony of my guest bedroom or from an umbrella-topped table situated on the stately front lawn where we sipped iced coffees and nibbled fresh-baked delicacies provided by Mrs. Donohue who had worked for Madge's family for years.

I loved my daily walks through the cobble stoned streets of the compact village and along the wind-blown wharf from which fishing boats launched their daily excursions. One of these tireless fishermen was Tom Wright whose family had resided in the village for as long as anyone could remember. Their baptismal records stretched as far back as the late 1700s, and Wright ancestors occupied a prominent section of the ancient cemetery located in front of the old stone church. Tom and his family lived above the general store that his wife Barbara ran. Their tall, pretty and perky teenaged daughter Sally was a sophomore at the state university and had recently returned home for summer vacation. I had enjoyed a number of pleasant conversations with Tom, and Sophie had become quite friendly with the warmhearted, gregarious Barbara during the two weeks we had been in the village. It was from Barbara that Sophie had learned that Sally had an admirer: no one other than Madge's recent college graduate son Edward.

I had grown quite fond of the quiet, studious Edward since he also had returned home for the summer. He had applied to a number of accounting firms for employment and had already gone to several promising interviews. While waiting to hear the results, he once more had resumed the summer jobs he had held since he was a boy: assisting

Barbara Wright in the store during the day and helping Tom unload his catch most evenings.

I had just lunched with Madge on the front lawn and was now sitting alone under the green striped awning listening to Madge's receding footsteps. I was thinking with a little apprehension about the boat ride Sophie had requested Tom Wright take us on this evening. To take my mind off that boat ride, I began proofreading the first act of my new play that I had finally finished dictating to Sophie only yesterday. Sophie had of course transcribed the script perfectly on the laptop she had brought with her and had printed the draft out this morning using Madge's printer. I heard Madge's voice in the distance and, looking up, saw her on the path that fronted her property greeting Sophie who had just returned from a walk "downtown," the inflated term the locals used to describe the few shops and other small businesses located about a twenty minute pleasant stroll from the Magill home. One quickly learned not to confuse this terminology with going "to town," that is, to the state capital about a sixty minute drive away.

"I'm off to the Laurence House to see that all is in order for the great man's appearance," Madge called out with a laugh, making sure that I heard her remark. I smiled to myself then assumed a solemnly care-worn expression and waved slowly and regally to Madge who then proceeded on her way. Both Madge and her son were becoming like family to me.

Sophie began ascending the front lawn. Halfway up, she suddenly stopped and turned round for a few seconds. Then I saw her shrug and continue walking up to my table.

"And a happy Saturday afternoon to you, Harry. Working hard, I see," Sophie quipped.

"Much too hard for this beautiful day," I laughed and put the printed pages aside. "I'll get back to correcting your numerous egregious typos after I return from the other amateurs."

Presenting me with a rude gesture I pretended not to see, Sophie sat down next to me at the table. "Despite what you say, boss, I think you're really enjoying working with those folks."

"As much as I hate to admit it, my dear Sophie, I must concede that you're right." When Madge had first asked me to attend a rehearsal of her little theatre group which concentrated on performing the works of Shakespeare, I cringed at the idea. After all, I was a Tony-nominated director with decades of work in the professional theatre. I had already more than paid my dues. Must I then, I had moaned silently to myself and very loudly to Sophie, be forced "to hear a robustious periwig-pated fellow tear a passion to tatters, to very rags," as a theatrically astute well-known royal Dane had put it.

However in deference to Madge's profound generosity to Sophie and me, I deigned to attend the meeting of the Laurence Little Players the first Saturday after we had arrived in Havenport. And I had been astonished.

Rather than overacting and mugging their Shakespearean scenes, the non-professional actors truthfully and honestly expressed their roles with a simplicity that did indeed "hold, as t'were, the mirror up to nature." They exhibited a few technical errors with the verse and could use a bit of assistance with their interpretations and staging, but the essentials were there. And they were a joy to watch.

The Laurence Little Players had been in existence for forty-seven years. They had been founded by Miss Annabelle Laurence, a grand old lady who was still leading the group. A patroness of the arts and a former teacher, the elderly Miss Laurence (she refused to be called by "the vulgar Ms." as she put it) was not only devoted to the works of the

Bard but to the elimination of social classes and prejudices. The heiress to a considerable family fortune, she had spent her adult life working to eliminate social barriers, fostering civil rights and providing educational opportunities for the economically and culturally disadvantaged. Madge had told us that most of Miss Laurence's fortune had been depleted by these noble endeavors, but she still persevered tirelessly for her causes. One of which was the Little Players.

The members of this community theatre group represented as diverse a social and economic spectrum as could be found in rural New England. I saw a retired state supreme court judge perform a comic Shakespearean scene with a farmer who had never finished fifth grade as her scene partner. The two would most probably never have met socially had they not been urged by Miss Laurence to join the Players. Madge Magill, the Yale archivist, was playing Cleopatra to the Antony of Joe Ginness, the town hall janitor. And so on, and so on. Throughout the years, strong friendships had been forged and social barriers had fallen due to the tireless work and egalitarian beliefs of this amazing woman.

Sophie joined me on my walk to the Laurence House, the fine old mansion where Annabelle Laurence lived and where the semi-weekly rehearsals of the Little Players were held. Practice sessions for the choral society she had founded were also accommodated there as well as the poetry writing, painting and sculpting classes she ran. All were held free of charge and frequented by people from all walks of life and economic strata. Today was the third rehearsal for me, and I looked forward to seeing how well the actors had incorporated my notes from last Thursday night's session into their work. Next Thursday night their scenes would be performed to the public. The lucky audience would not only receive free admission to the show but a complimentary potluck supper after the performance prepared by the Players.

As we neared our destination, Sophie suddenly stopped walking and turned around rapidly looking back behind her with a strange expression on her face.

"Anything the matter?" I asked.

She was silent for several more moments before she turned to me and said, "I may be going bananas, Harry, but for the last few days I've felt that someone was following me. It's not like those damned cameramen who constantly pursued us after Brookfield. It's a different sort of feeling. And, I'm ashamed to say, it's giving me a bit of the creeps."

"Sophie, I don't see anyone behind us now. Do you?"

"No, dammit, I don't. And I've never spotted anyone. But I still feel it in my bones that someone in hiding is following me and watching me. It happened twice today as I was coming back from downtown."

Although I was tempted to pooh-pooh her feeling, I didn't and merely said, "Well, we'll both be on the lookout for this person and confront him when we find him. But let's not let it spoil our holiday. What do you say?"

"When you're right, you're right, Harry," she said with a brave smile. "I'm really turning into a cream puff in my old age, aren't I?" With a laugh, we turned into the lane to the Laurence House where we spent an enjoyable two hours.

If I had known then how dramatically all our lives were soon to change, I would have embraced the pleasures I derived from this rehearsal session even more fully.

AS THE AMATEUR ACTORS PERFORMED their short Shakespearean scenes and monologues, I complimented them in turn on their considerable progress. However, each afforded me an opportunity to teach them all a bit more about the finer points of acting in general and performing the Bard in particular. Sophie no doubt would quickly add that it also allowed me the opportunity to show off, but I digress.

Here's an example of the good work achieved at that rehearsal. Nora and Noah Benson performed the dramatic interchange between Othello and his wife's handmaiden from the final scene of the tragedy. It begins when Othello confesses to Desdemona's murder because he believes she was unfaithful to him. Emilia denies that slanderous charge.

OTHELLO

She's like a liar gone to burning hell.

'Twas I that killed her.

EMILIA

Oh, the more angel she,

And you the blacker devil!

OTHELLO

She turned to folly, and she was a whore.

EMILIA

Thou dost belie her, and thou art a devil.

OTHELLO

She was false as water.

EMILIA

Thou art rash as fire,

To say that she was false. Oh, she was heavenly true!

"Good work, both of you," I complimented after the applause from the other enthusiastic actors had abated. "Let me add a further note that should benefit all of you in working on Shakespearean text. It is another indication of how masterfully the playwright used language to help develop characterization. But to understand this, you'll need to understand the difference between 'you' and 'thou' in Elizabethan English. Can anyone tell me the difference?"

"Aren't 'thou' and 'thee' and 'thy' and 'thine' and all those just old fashioned, sorta highfalutin words only used in poetry?" asked Ray Gross the plain talking farmer in the group. "Sure, I only come across 'thou' in the Bible and Shakespeare," concurred RoseMarie Farrell, the attractive mother of six, grandmother of thirteen, and great-grandmother of three.

A benevolent smile appeared on my lips. Sophie would have termed it one of smug satisfaction, but I digress.

"You're right that the only second person pronoun we now use in English is 'you.' But that wasn't always the case. Just as today there are two forms for the second person pronoun in modern French (tu/vous) and German (du/Sie), English once had these distinctions as well. To address an intimate, a friend, or one of lower status a speaker would automatically use the informal, the personal 'thou.' To address a respected personage or one of higher social class, a speaker would use the more formal 'you.'

"So addressing the high ranking general Othello, the lowly maid Emilia would automatically use the formal 'you.' And she does so in her first line even though he has just confessed to murdering her beloved mistress:

> EMILIA
> Oh, the more angel she,
> And YOU the blacker devil!

"But, after he besmirches Desdemona's honor, Emilia loses all sense of decorum and inbred protocol and illustrates how much she now despises him by shouting out to all who can hear that his infamy has divested him of all the respect and deference automatically bestowed on his social standing by saying to him:

> THOU dost belie her, and THOU art a devil!
> THOU art rash as fire

"The Elizabethan audience would have instinctively understood these niceties of language and would have been shocked at Emilia's use of the informal 'thou' to address a superior. So, Shakespeare has provided the actor playing Emilia with a wealth of information about the degree of her hatred at this moment, and it is up to you, Nora, to find an equivalent today in expressing the depth of your loathing of Noah."

"Only in the scene, of course," interjected Sophie.

But I digress.

Chapter 3

Returning home, I walked with Madge, and Sophie walked alongside Barbara Wright, also a member of the Laurence Little Players, who with her acting partner Patrolman Robby Donohue had performed her difficult scene from *King Lear* surprisingly well. I noticed Barbara and Sophie were engaged in a rather animated discussion as they walked several steps ahead of us.

Sophie and I had a light supper with Madge before leaving her and walking down to the wharf where Tom Wright would be waiting for us. On the way, I asked Sophie why Barbara had seemed so agitated when we had left Laurence House.

"Barbara told me she's nervous about how quickly the relationship between Sally and Edward seems to be progressing. She thinks Edward is becoming much too serious about her daughter, and this worries her. She and Tom confronted Sally about this last night. Sally told them not to worry, that she agreed with her parents that she was too young to get serious and settle down. She said that she would talk to Edward about this matter on their date tonight. Although Barbara was still concerned, she told me that she felt somewhat relieved by their conversation."

"Perhaps we should talk to Edward ourselves," I suggested. "He does seem to like us, and I think he respects our opinions."

"Maybe we should do just that," Sophie responded as we reached the wharf. She greeted Tom warmly and after a comforting smile to me and a reassuring squeeze of my arm, she took Tom's hand as he helped her into his boat. Tom had kindly consented to take us out on his smaller private motorboat rather **than** the larger one he used for fishing. I still had not quite gotten used to the lingering fishy odor that emanated from the trawler.

Sophie had to do quite a lot of convincing before I had consented to take this sunset cruise with her. I must admit to a phobia about boats stemming from a childhood incident with my father when we both nearly drowned. Over the years I had managed to sail on large cruise ships but still had a lingering hesitation about the smaller variety.

However, since I trusted Tom's ability as a sailor and the June evening was so perfect and the sea so calm, with a steely smile I followed Sophie into the boat. After donning life jackets, we cast off.

As the sun began to descend and the gentle breezes ruffled my hair, I let out an expansive sigh and slowly began to relax and enjoy the experience. The coastline was transcendently beautiful. The rugged cliffs above us turned golden as the sun grew lower in the sky. We spied several caves that glistened mysteriously as we passed by. Tom maneuvered the lazy currents masterfully, and when he began to sing softly an old sea chantey in his pleasant baritone voice the scene became truly idyllic to me.

I thought of Belinda whom I hadn't seen for several months but would meet again in London in July. All indications were that the disorders from which she had suffered in Brookfield were now being controlled, and I could foresee a real future with her once again.

As Sophie took out the bottle of champagne and three glasses she had tucked into her ever present tote bag, she suddenly shuddered, quickly looked up and squinting her eyes said, "Look, there's a man watching us from that cliff in front of us. Is he holding something? I can't see."

We all looked in that direction. I detected the figure Sophie had spotted, "My God, it looks like he's pointing a rifle at us." The sound was unbelievably loud and echoed and re-echoed around the cliffs as the bullet found its target.

Chapter 4

"Yet who would have thought the old man to have had so much blood in him?"

I couldn't get Lady Macbeth's horrifying question out of my head as I stared dumbfounded at the writhing body of Tom Wright. So much blood had gushed out of him immediately after he had been shot that it was difficult for me at first to ascertain which part of his body had been hit. Sophie had immediately stood up and rushed to his side.

Her movements had caused the small boat to wobble dangerously. Holding on for dear life, I shouted to her, "Stay down, Sophie, for God's sake. He'll get you too!"

"It's all right, Harry. He's no longer there. He's gone."

I turned around once again and saw that Sophie was right. After firing that one shot, the man with the rifle had vanished from the top of the cliff. He must have gone back down the other side.

Sophie was now saying something else to me. Still pretty much in a daze, I turned back to her trying to give this sudden nightmare my full attention. "Harry, I think I saw a first-aid kit under the pile of life jackets. Get if for me, please. We need something to stanch this bleeding."

First aid kit? First aid kit? Ah, there it was. Suddenly confronted with that uncompromising scarlet cross emblazoned across the white metal box, my head seemed to clear a bit, and I opened the kit and dutifully handed it to Sophie. She had already ripped open Tom's shirt, and the gaping wound oozing blood made me feel queasy again.

Yet I wanted to be of assistance. Taking my cell phone from my pocket, I told Sophie, "I'll try to call for help. Let's see if I can reach 911." Having learned how spotty cell phone reception had proven to be in the environs of Havenport, I was not terribly optimistic that my phone would work this far out from shore. As I waited, I desperately prayed that the "Can you hear me?" man testing the reliability of his phone company's wireless network in all those TV commercials had somehow miraculously visited this stretch of the Atlantic wearing water wings and flippers.

I then heard Sophie muttering to herself. "Now let's see what I remember from that first aid course I took thirty years ago. Thirty years! Holey moley! All right. Now I've put on these plastic gloves to avoid contact with the victim's blood. Check. Now I'm pressing a sterile gauze patch directly on the wound. Check . . ."

My phone for a moment seemed to connect. I held my breath.

"Now I keep the pressure constant for at least five minutes. This allows the blood to clot preventing additional bleeding. Check . . ."

No, I was mistaken. The damn phone would just not work out here in the middle of the ocean, or wherever the hell we were. How could we contact help?

"Harry," Sophie called breaking into my incipient nervous breakdown. "Help me lift Tom up. I remember it's vital to raise the wound above heart level. At least I think I remember that."

I tried the best I could to keep the boat from rocking too much as I raised Tom to a higher sitting position at the front of the boat but still leaning against Sophie. He then looked directly into my eyes and seemed to be trying to communicate with me. He touched the cell phone I was holding and seemed to shake his head.

"Ray . . . Ray . . . Joe," he seemed to be saying. "Ray Joe Stern."

"Ray Joe Stern?" I repeated like an idiot.

Seeing my blank face, Tom turned his head to Sophie and weakly pointing to the back of the boat repeated "Ray Joe" to her.

"Oh, he means radio, Harry. There must be one over there in the stern, the back of the boat. Is that right, Tom?"

He infinitesimally nodded his assent and then began moaning once again. I moved as quickly as I dared and located several watertight bags next to the outboard motor. In the second one I opened, I found what looked like a small handheld gizmo that sort of resembled a walkie talkie. Hoping this was some kind of marine radio, I pushed the center button causing the little screen in the front to glow. There were other buttons each apparently accessing a different channel. I pressed each one in turn and called out, "Help. Can you help us? We're on Tom Wright's boat, and Tom has been shot. Help us, someone, please. Maypole!"

No, that wasn't it. What was that distress call I wanted to use? Somewhere from the bowels of my memory banks, probably from some old John Wayne war movie I had not seen for decades, it erupted out of me: "Mayday!"

All this time, the boat had been slowly moving in a straight line farther and farther away from shore. As I was now sitting next to the motor, I hesitantly moved the lever or handle or rudder or whatever it was, as I had seen Tom do. And the gods be praised, somehow or other I managed slowly to turn the boat around heading back, I hoped, in the direction of the land we could no longer see. And all the while, I continued pushing buttons on that gizmo and calling out for help. And all the while, Sophie continued to do her best to minister to the severely injured man she held against her. And all the while, it incrementally grew darker and darker. And all of a sudden, we heard a disconcerting grinding sound, and the boat lurched to a stop.

"Now what?" I growled. Although the engine was still operating, something was preventing us from moving. I looked over the side of the boat and saw that we were situated in the midst of a greenish brown mass of vegetation that extended on all sides of us as far as I could see in the diminished light.

"Look, Sophie." I noticed that the pitch of my voice was unnaturally high. "There's some sort of seaweed all around us."

"Harry, that looks like kelp."

"Kelp, shmelp," I helpfully uttered. "Is that what's keeping us from moving?"

"It could very well be. It can grow in what they call underwater forests, and that could be what we're stuck in. They can grow to be hundreds of feet long. I bet the blades of the motor's propeller are all tangled up in this kelp forest."

"Well, that's really great," I sputtered. "So how are we going to disentangle ourselves?"

"Well, Harry . . ." Sophie paused. My heart sank as she hesitatingly continued. "Do you think you could possibly . . . get into the water . . . and make an assessment of how bad the situation is?"

It was amazing how quickly my forehead became drenched with perspiration. Sophie looked at the horror in my eyes and softly said,

"I know your problem with the ocean and with boats, Harry, I do. I'd gladly go in myself, but I don't think Tom should be moved in any way right now. He's looking and sounding much worse." Indeed, Tom's eyes were now closed, and his groaning had grown more intense the last few moments.

So, I guess I would just have to climb overboard and get into that green goop. After all, I did have a life jacket on. So, I probably wouldn't drown. I probably wouldn't suffocate when the seaweed (sorry, kelp) got hold of me and pulled me underwater. I probably wouldn't be cut into shreds by the propeller blades when I got too near them.

I'm sure I could have come up with many more dire fates that probably wouldn't be in store for me had not a crackling sound scared the life out of both of us and had we not heard the most glorious voice imaginable say the most glorious words imaginable. No, it was not an angel from on high with gossamer wings materializing out of the ether to lead us to our eternal reward. It was even better. It was the voice coming from the radio of a Lieutenant Harold Mossgrove of the U.S. Coast Guard calmly stating that he had heard my distress call and that his cutter with a medical technician on board was on its way to rescue us.

As I sat down next to Sophie, I heard what she was quietly saying in Tom's ear. "Don't worry, Tom. They're coming to help us. They're coming to help you. A doctor is coming, and he'll fix you right up. I know he will. Oh, Tom, I'm so sorry you were hurt. I think that bullet was meant for me, and you just somehow got in the way. You see, someone's been following me, and I think he must be the one who shot that rifle. I think it was meant for me, Tom, not you. And I'm so, so sorry."

Tom then opened his eyes and looked deeply into Sophie's. Then he opened his mouth and tried to speak. It was now difficult for him to formulate the words he wanted to say, and it was extremely difficult for me to understand the meaning of the sounds that he managed weakly to make. I think I heard him say, "I know . . . I know who . . . . Who . . . I know . . ." He tried to utter more sounds but seemed to be unable to do so. It looked to me that his lips were trying to form a plosive sound like "pihh" or "bihh." He then coughed deeply for several moments. Sophie wiped away the blood he was now coughing up. He tried to speak again. This time he turned to me and said what sounded like "You know . . . . Who . . ." He coughed once more. Then still looking at me, he said what sounded like "Eck" or maybe "Ake" (perhaps it was ache?) Then he weakly raised his finger and pointed at me as he repeated several times: "Aches . . . Tooth . . . Aches . . . Tooth . . . Tooths . . . Aches . . . ."

Then the sounds stopped for good.

Chapter 5

The events of the next hour or so passed by in a blur. I can only recall sporadic sounds and images: the basso profundo horn blast of the coast guard cutter and its blinding beam of light as it blazed a swath through the darkness towards us; the hurried, hushed words spoken as the crew members desperately attempted to resuscitate the limp body, and the sudden, impenetrable silence that followed the realization of their failure to do so. I remember the tears in the eyes of Lieutenant Mossgrove and the catch in his voice as he softly whispered to no one in particular, "Tom and Barbara were at my wedding."

And then somehow we were at the familiar wharf where the entire village, it seemed, had gathered to bid a tearful farewell to their well-liked neighbor and friend. Even in the dim light, we could discern the looks of grief and incomprehension in the red-eyed faces of the people we passed. As Patrolman Donohue began to lead Sophie and me through the crowd, she broke away and ran to Barbara who was protectively surrounded by a number of her fellow Little Players.

Enfolding the pale and suddenly fragile-looking Barbara in her arms, Sophie managed to have a few quiet words with her. The noise of the cutter's engine starting again prevented me from overhearing what was said. Then Barbara was helped aboard, and the boat carrying her husband's corpse sped off for the trip to the state capital.

"She shouldn't have gone alone," I said to Sophie after she had rejoined the patrolman and me. "Sally should have gone with her."

"Barbara just told me that Sally's not home yet from her date with Edward," Sophie replied obviously upset. "She had tried to phone Sally after receiving word from the police but only got her voice mail. She didn't want her to hear about her father's death in that way, so she asked me to go back to their place and wait there until Sally got home to break the news to her as gently as possible."

"I think it would be better if we all went over to the station so I can take down exactly what happened," Robby Donohue said to us in his soft-spoken manner. We had met Robby several times in Madge's kitchen when he had visited his mother and had of course seen him rehearse with the Little Players. He appeared to be a very nice, very polite young man. His unassuming bearing seemed rather surprising for a policeman. But just about every person we had met in Havenport had seemed equally pleasant, kind and friendly. This made the horrifying events on Tom's boat even more unbelievable and shocking.

Sophie was about to reply to Robby's words when the sounds of rapid footsteps made us all turn our heads. Madge Magill was frantically running towards us followed closely by her housekeeper Mrs. Donohue.

"Oh, my dears. My poor, poor dears," she cried as she first hugged Sophie and then me. "We just heard the terrible news on the car radio. How are you? Are you all right?"

"I'm really not sure, Madge," I responded. "This whole business has been such a shock."

"Of course, of course it has. What exactly happened? Why would anyone want to kill Tom Wright, of all people?"

"Madge, I don't think that bullet was meant for Tom . . ." Sophie's voice cracked as she began to reply.

Before she could continue, Robby gently interrupted. "I really think it would be better all around if you and Mr. Hunt didn't talk about this now to anyone. So, I think the three of us should go downtown to the station. I'll make sure it doesn't take too long."

"Robby, I promised Barbara that I'll wait at her place until Sally comes home, and I am not going to break that promise." I could see that Sophie was beginning to lose whatever composure she had been able to maintain. Her voice was becoming louder, and the defiant stubbornness in the set of her features was unmistakable. I feared an imminent confrontation between Sophie and the young man. If that happened, I knew from past experience that Sophie would be the odds-on favorite to emerge victorious.

Luckily, the patrolman's mother defused the situation by coming up to him and saying in her sensible, comforting tone, "Now, Robby, you can understand that Miss Sophie and Mr. Hunt have gone to hell and back tonight. I'm sure you can bend the rules a bit and get all you need to hear from them at the Wright's apartment as well as you could at the police station. I'll make all of us a nice cup of tea there while you do your job. We'll all wait for Sally to come home and do our best to console the poor child when she returns. All right, my darling boy?"

As Robby began to blush a little, Madge said to him, "I'd like to be there as well when Edward drops Sally off. If they haven't heard the news yet, I know it will be a terrible shock for him too. He's been so close to the whole family since he was a boy. They should be coming back pretty soon. They were only going to catch an early movie. How about it, Robby?"

All eyes then turned to the young policeman who after a moment's hesitation finally sighed and quietly said, "Well, I guess I have no choice. But I do need to get your statements, Mr. Hunt and Miss Xerxes, before the state police get here and take over." He paused and then said with a slight smile, "And I think we can all use a cup of ma's tea."

"Or perhaps something a wee bit stronger?" I suggested. "For medicinal purposes only, of course."

"Of course," Sophie and Robby both said this phrase simultaneously and then awkwardly smiled a bit at each other. They each seemed relieved that the potential standoff had been resolved so amicably.

Although it would have taken us no more than five or six minutes to walk to the Wrights' general store from the wharf, after Robby had quietly but capably asked the crowd to go back to their homes, he drove Sophie and me there. Madge and Mrs. Donohue followed in the latter's car which had been hurriedly parked near the wharf.

A few minutes later, we had used the key Barbara had handed to Sophie at the wharf and had climbed the stairs above the store, turned on the lights in the comfortable yet now eerily silent living room where Robby, Sophie and I sat down. Madge and Mrs. Donohue proceeded to the kitchen and closed the door behind them.

Patrolman Donohue had just recorded our full names and addresses in his policeman's notebook (It looked a lot like the one Sophie always carried with her.) when we heard the cheery whistle of a tea kettle from the kitchen followed soon by the two ladies briskly entering the living room or "parlor" as they all called it. Mrs. Donohue carried a full tray which she placed on the coffee table in front of us.

"Now this will only take a minute, Robby," she said with a smile, "and it will make us all feel a great deal better. It's my famous recipe for a toasty hot toddy, Mr. Hunt, guaranteed to soothe both body and soul."

Humming to herself, Mrs. Donohue first coated the bottom of each of the five tea cups on the tray with a teaspoon of honey. She then squeezed fresh lemon juice into the cups.

"Before I add the nice hot tea I just brewed, you'll have to find where Tom kept his spirits, Robby. Maybe some brandy for the ladies, and whisky or rum for Mr. Hunt?"

"I think he kept them in here," Robby volunteered as he walked over to an old wooden desk in the corner of the room. Rolling up the top, he revealed a healthy assortment of bottles. "Here's some brandy. And what's your pleasure, Mr. Hunt?" An ounce or so of brandy poured into the cups for Madge and Mrs. Donohue and a larger amount of rum for both Sophie and me (Why ruin the good and quite expensive Scotch I saw there by diluting it?) followed by the steaming tea, a brisk stir, a cinnamon stick in each cup, a few sips, and we all were feeling at least a little better. Taking their cups back into the kitchen, Madge and her housekeeper left us to answer Robby's further questions.

Taking another sip of his tea (Robby had refrained from adding anything stronger since he was "on duty.") he began by asking us a series of background questions "for the record, you understand." Why had we come to Havenport? How long had we been in Havenport? Whom had we met in Havenport? Had we had any unpleasantness, any confrontations, made any enemies in Havenport? Had we any enemies that we could think of outside of Havenport?

Sophie and I fielded these questions easily enough, but they began, I thought, to hint at the possibility that Tom Wright had not been the intended victim. I brought this up to Robby immediately.

"Are your questions suggesting that the killer meant to shoot Sophie or me rather than Tom, Robby?"

"I'm not suggesting anything right now, Mr. Hunt. I'm just collecting information. It seems to me that there are only four possibilities. First, the shooting was some sort of bizarre accident. The guy with the rifle might have been skeet shooting, or shooting at birds, or some such thing and never intended to hit any of you."

"That really seems hardly likely, Robby," Sophie remarked. "When I saw that bastard on the cliff, I'm sure he was deliberately pointing his rifle at us."

"That certainly was what I thought when I turned around and saw him up there," I said.

"Was there any possibility that the fella could have been just joking, not intending to hurt anyone, and the joke just went terribly wrong, do you think?"

"Using real bullets? I hardly think so, Robby."

"Of course it would seem that you're right, Mr. Hunt," Robby said. "It's just so unlikely, so strange for this sort of thing to take place in Havenport. I can't remember anything like this ever happening here, ever, and I've lived in Havenport all my life. I can't imagine any of the people who live here deliberately doing anything like this, and, especially, doing it to Tom Wright."

"Well, like it or not, someone did do it." Sophie was getting riled up again.

"Right, but was Tom the intended target?" Robby asked.

"Well, why should someone want to kill either Sophie or me? Everyone we've met in our two weeks here has treated us with nothing but kindness itself."

"Have you seen any strangers in the village while you've been here, any outsiders, Mr. Hunt?" Robby seemed to be clutching at straws.

"No, I don't think so. Everyone is so close-knit here. A stranger would stick out like a sore thumb."

"Right, right." Robby paused to take another sip from his cup. It seemed a good idea, so Sophie and I both followed suit. I secretly wished now that there had been even more rum in the tea, or perhaps less tea in the rum.

"Miss Xerxes," Robby put his cup down again and turned to Sophie. "I believe I heard you say to Mrs. Magill that you thought (How did you put it?) that the bullet was not intended for Tom. Isn't that what you said?"

There was another pause and then Sophie answered, "Yes, you're right. That's what I said."

"Why did you say that, may I ask?"

She took a big breath and then said, "You may think I've lost it, Robby; I know Harry here does." I began to speak, but Sophie silenced me with a look and continued. "But I feel sure that someone, some creep has been following me for the last several days. I've felt his presence behind me, but every time I turned around, he had vanished. So I have no idea who this person is or why he's doing it, but I know deep inside me that some sinister guy has been lurking around wanting to harm me in some way and finally tried to do so from the top of that cliff. Only poor, sweet Tom somehow got in the way."

Tears were beginning to form in Sophie's eyes. But before I could do anything to help, we heard a knock at the apartment's kitchen door. We heard one of the ladies in the kitchen go to the door and open it.

Although the door connecting the living room to the kitchen was closed, we could clearly hear the voice of Edward Magill.

"Oh, hi, Mrs. Donohue. Oh, mom, you're here too. Is Sally still up? I'd like to have a few words with her."

Chapter 6

"What gives, Harry?" Sophie whispered. I could think of no better response than to shrug my shoulders in bewilderment. We had expected Edward and Sally to return together from their date. So why had he turned up alone asking to speak to her?

Sophie and I weren't the only ones to find this odd. Robby then quietly asked under his breath what I assumed was a rhetorical question, "You don't think she's been here the whole time, do you?" He then added, "I'd better check out the rest of the apartment." As Sophie and I started to rise, he said with a trace of caution in his voice, "You two better wait here for now."

So we waited. Waited and listened. We listened as the hall light switch clicked on, and then we listened to the sound of Robby's footsteps heading down the hallway. We listened as Robby opened one bedroom door, clicked on the light, paused and then proceeded to the far bedroom, Sally's bedroom. Its door creaked open. Its light switch clicked on. And then there was silence.

"Harry," Sophie worriedly began, "you don't think . . . ?" Before she could complete her question, Edward Magill quickly entered from the kitchen followed by his mother and Mrs. Donohue.

"Mr. Hunt," Edward said upon seeing me. "What's going on here? I only want to see Sally for a minute. Has something happened?"

"I'm afraid so, Edward." The tone of Patrolman Donohue's voice had changed as he re-entered the living room.

"What do you mean, Robby? Where's Sally?" We all noticed that Edward's tone had altered as well. His voice had taken on a slight but noticeably tremulous quality.

"That's what I'd like to ask you, Edward," Robby responded quietly. "When did you last see her?"

There was now a steely hardness in the patrolman's eyes which made me again rise from my chair and say, "Robby, did you find . . . ?" He silenced me with a small but clear hand gesture, and I quickly resumed my seat.

The several moments of silence that then elapsed made me feel terribly apprehensive. The looks on both young men's faces were both so supercharged that I was forced to turn my eyes elsewhere. I looked at Sophie and saw that she was staring at something behind Robby's back. I followed her gaze and saw that he was holding behind him what looked like a folded-up clear plastic bag. There was something in the bag. Something pink and sparkly. Was I seeing correctly? I turned back to Sophie with a questioning look but noticed that she was now focused on Edward's hands. When I looked down, I saw that they were now held in front of him fiercely gripping the back of a chair. The expression "white knuckles" couldn't have been more accurate. In fact, his entire hands had now turned such a shade of ghostly white (I assume he was cutting off the circulation of blood to them by squeezing the chair so tightly) that a small, semi-circular purplish-red spot on the back of his left hand (Was it a birthmark?) became very noticeable.

The silence continued and the tension between the two of them grew even more palpable until Robby finally repeated slowly, quietly and not unkindly, "When did you last see Sally, Edward?"

"Uh, a couple of hours ago, I imagine. When I left her at the movie theater. What's happened, Robby?"

Instead of answering, the patrolman asked, "You left her at the movies? Why was that, Edward?"

A slight flush was spreading over Edward's face as he haltingly said, "Well, I don't really see why it's any of your business, but we had what I guess you could call a few words after the film ended, and Sally told me she'd rather not go home with me. She said she'd get one of her girl friends to pick her up. I waited while she made a call on her cell, and when she had arranged the ride home I drove off."

"Robby, I don't think . . ." Mrs. Donohue began, but her son interrupted.

"Just a minute, ma, please. Edward, how many cell phones does Sally have?"

"Why, just one, I think. Why?"

"And if I remember correctly it's a rather special-looking one, isn't it?"

"Yes, I guess so. It's the one I gave her as a present last Christmas after she had lost her previous one."

"And she used that phone to call for a ride home?"

"Yes. Yes, she did. So what?" Edward's flush had now extended completely down his neck.

I then recalled noticing Sally using the cell phone in question last week and teasing her about it. She had giggled attractively and had admitted that "I guess I'm just a girly-girl at heart, Mr. Hunt. So much for all the progress made by women's lib." That silly phone was bright pink in color and was festooned with fake diamonds and was now, I was sure, in that plastic bag that Robby held behind his back.

"I was just curious, Edward," Robby softly replied. Sophie and I both noticed that Robby then unobtrusively placed the bag into his back pocket.

"Mom, would you or someone please tell me what's going on?" Edward pleaded.

"Edward, Sally's father was shot this evening," Madge said softly.

"What? Oh my God. Tom?" Edward looked astounded and quickly asked her, "How is he?"

"I'm afraid he's gone, Edward." Madge put her arm around her son.

"Oh, my God." Edward's voice could now barely be heard.

"Robby," Madge turned to the patrolman, "I'm going to go home now with my son. This has all been a terrible shock to all of us. I trust that meets with your approval."

I was surprised when Robby nodded his assent to Madge. She then began to lead Edward from the room. He resisted a bit saying, "But, mom, I need to see Sally and help her with this."

"We don't know where Sally is, honey. Let's get a bit of rest now. We could both use it."

Mrs. Donohue then started to follow them into the kitchen, but Madge said to her, "We'll take our own car home, Edna. No need for you to bother. It's parked outside, Edward?"

"Yes, mom, but I'd rather . . ."

"We'll see you later at the house," Madge said to Sophie and me as she led her son through the kitchen, closing the outside door soundly behind them.

We sat like statues for a moment or two trying to assess all that had just happened. Then just as Sophie and I were opening our mouths to speak, Robby beat us to it by saying to his mother, "Ma, I think it would be best if you went home as well. It's really getting late, and I bet you can be of some help to Mrs. Magill and Edward."

Mrs. Donohue agreed and after bidding us good night and giving Robby a peck on the cheek, she left the three of us alone in the empty (I strongly hoped) apartment. Her carriage and walk reflected the strain that we all had experienced this terrible evening.

"I would like to finish up the questioning if you wouldn't mind. I promise it won't take too much longer. I know what you've gone through, but let's get it over with as quickly as we can so we all can get some sleep."

Robby's tone was so sincerely apologetic and he looked as stunned as we were after this bizarre turn of events with Edward that we consented and listened as he mumbled, "So where were we?" while consulting the notes he had taken in his notebook. "Oh, yes, I had told you there were only four possible explanations that I can think of for the shooting in the boat. The first was that it was a strange accident or some joke that, that . . ."

"That misfired?" I piped in. (Bad pun intended) "I think we can exclude that theory."

"Yes, probably," Robby seemed to agree. "The next possibility is that Tom Wright was the intended victim, but as far as I know he hadn't an enemy in the world. That only leaves . . ."

"That the bastard wanted to kill Harry or me and missed," Sophie said with a slight shudder.

"You both have received a lot of notice in the media since your book came out, Mr. Hunt. There is the possibility that some nutcase is skulking around wanting to cash in on his own fifteen minutes of fame by doing in a celebrity. I could cite you case after case."

"I certainly can think of many, myself," I concurred grimly.

"And the invisible man who has been following Miss Xerxes the past few days would seem to lead us in that direction, don't you think?"

There was a pause as we digested what Robby had just said. He then continued, "After I get all the information we need from the two of you, I would like to suggest, off the record, as a friend, that you might be a hell of a lot better off leaving Havenport earlier than you had planned. If there's some fruitcake living or hanging out around here who has it in for either or both of you, I wouldn't give him more of an opportunity. Believe me, there's lots more protection for you in a big city with a large police presence than in our little village. Nothing happened to you for the last year until you came here, right? Think about it. Please, just think about it."

The last remark was directed specifically to Sophie whose whole demeanor now made it obvious that the idea of running away from a fight was not at all to her liking.

"We'll think about it, Robby," I interjected. "I promise."

"Thank you, Mr. Hunt. Now, let's get the rest of my questions finished off. Why were the two of you out in Tom's boat to begin with?"

"I take the blame for that too," Sophie replied. "It was my idiotic idea that if I could get the boss out for a beautiful sunset cruise with people he liked, that would go a long way in helping him deal with the problem he has with boats. That certainly turned out to be one of my better ideas." Her eyes began to grow watery again, so I crossed over to Sophie, sat beside her and patted her hand reassuringly.

"With people he liked," Robby repeated. "So you liked Tom Wright, did you, Mr. Hunt? How well did you know him?"

"Tom was one of the first people I met when we got to Havenport, and I enjoyed talking to him," I answered.

"A local fisherman seems a bit of an unusual type for a big city guy like you to associate with."

"Well, you're right, Robby. I've never really met anybody like Tom before," I said. "And it was his commonsensical, practical, honest way of looking at life that interested me. At first, I thought he'd be a good model for one of the characters in the new play I'm trying to write, but then I really started enjoying our conversations so much that I made it a point to spend some time with him most evenings after he returned home. It became a practice that we both enjoyed."

"And what did you two talk about, may I ask?"

"Well, we first talked about his life but, strangely enough, soon we almost exclusively talked about mine."

"About your life?" Robby seemed surprised.

"Yes, and about literature, about the theatre and plays, a lot about plays. Tom hadn't had much of an education, and he deeply regretted that. He was very interested in all I could tell him about the theatre and especially about the works of Shakespeare. Because Barbara was currently working on a scene from *King Lear* with the Little Players, we started with that and began to discuss the play in great detail. He took a paperback edition of *Lear* out with him on his fishing boat, and we went over what he had read each evening when we got together."

"Shakespeare, huh? What do you know?" Robby scratched his head once or twice and then turned the topic to the particular details of the shooting. He was surprised that we had strayed so far from the normal shipping lanes to have gotten entangled in the kelp forest. He dutifully recorded in his notebook Tom's last words but made no comments about them. From the clear descriptions Sophie was able to give him about the cliff from which the rifle was fired, Robby was pretty sure that it was the one the locals called "Old Blighty." He told us he and the state police would investigate the site the next morning.

After a few more questions, Robby closed his notebook. "I'm sorry to have put both of you through so much, but it had to be done." He stifled a yawn as he looked at his watch. "Jeez, it's after eleven. Time for us all to get some sleep. Do you want me to drive you back to Mrs. Magill's place?"

"Robby, I told Barbara I'd wait here till Sally came home, and that's what I'm going to do," Sophie said. "But, Harry, why don't you go with Robby? You might as well sleep in your own bed. I'll call you if anything happens."

I was delighted to hear Sophie's suggestion but thought it appropriate to ask, "Are you sure, Sophie? I don't want to leave you here all alone." I'm afraid my delivery of that line was not terribly convincing.

"I'm sure, Harry," Sophie laughed a little. "You two boys go on now. I'll be fine."

"Well, if you're sure," I said rapidly rising and slipping on my jacket. As I started to follow the patrolman, I happened to glance out the living room window. What I saw made me suddenly say, "On second thought, Robby, I've decided to stay here with Sophie. Sally must be coming home soon. Thanks anyway."

Robby gave me an odd look but then said, "Suit yourself, Mr. Hunt. Good night to you both. I'll speak to you tomorrow."

I walked him out and then returned to Sophie as she said, "That's very nice of you, Harry, but there's no need for both of us . . ."

I interrupted her while looking out the window once again. "Sophie, I just now saw someone hiding behind that tree outside. I think he's still there."

Sophie's voice turned to a whisper as she joined me and looked out. "Who's hiding out there, Harry? Can you see?"

I paused a moment before I quietly said, "I'm sure it's Edward Magill."

Chapter 7

"Edward? He went home with Madge only about forty minutes ago."

"Well, he's back now," I whispered while closing the living room drapes a bit more. "Don't you see him there crouching behind that oak tree?"

"I see someone, and I think you're right. It is Edward. What's he doing there?"

"He seems to be watching Robby's police car, waiting for him to drive off. Maybe he's come back here to talk to us without Robby's presence," I suggested.

We heard the car drive off and surreptitiously watched Edward rise to a standing position then look around him nervously.

"I feel like an idiot spying on Edward like this," Sophie said. "If he wants to come in and talk to us, it's because he trusts us. He might feel less inclined to do so if he catches sight of us peering at him behind a pair of curtains."

I was about to concur with Sophie when I saw Edward move not towards the front of the general store and the staircase to the Wrights' upstairs apartment but, instead, soundlessly go around the back of the store and out of our line of sight.

"Where's he going?" I asked.

"I would think he's headed for the shed behind the store where Barbara keeps extra supplies, tools, and the like. I went back there with her once when she was doing inventory."

"It's almost midnight. Why would Edward want to go back there now, Sophie? And how could he get in? I suppose the shed is locked."

"Yes, it is. In fact the key to the shed is right here on the ring of keys Barbara handed to me." Sophie retrieved the set of keys from her tote bag. "See, here it is clearly marked."

"Edward works for Barbara in the store during the day, Sophie. Maybe he has his own set of keys."

We then heard through the open window the faint but unmistakable clanking of a metal door being rolled up. "I guess Edward does have a spare key, Sophie. What does he want in the storage shed?"

"Harry, I'm beginning to have a really bad feeling about this. Did you buy what Edward said? He sure seemed nervous when he told Robby—how did he put it?—that he and Sally 'had words' after the movie."

"Their disagreement must have been major enough for Sally not to want Edward to drive her home. I wonder what it was about?" I mused.

"Well, Barbara said that Sally was going to tell Edward he was getting too serious. I wonder if that's why they had 'words.'"

"But Edward is such a quiet, studious, calm young man. None of this behavior seems typical of him."

"Don't they always say that it's the nice quiet types who turn out to be . . ." Sophie paused midway through her observation.

"Serial killers?" I finished her remark.

"Yeah. That's what they always seem to say." We both looked at each other for a moment. Then Sophie asked me, "Harry, did you see what Robby had in that plastic bag he was hiding behind his back?"

"It certainly looked like that pink cell phone of Sally's."

"Right. The one Edward said Sally used to call her friend. Well, from my angle, it sure looked like the LCD screen on the front of the phone was broken. I once dropped my cell phone, and it was the little glass screen that smashed and had to be replaced. Until then I couldn't use the phone."

"Are you sure that's what you saw, Sophie? I didn't notice that."

"I'm pretty positive. Robby must have found the phone in Sally's bedroom when he went back there. I'm going in there to take a look myself."

"I'll go with you," I said.

"No, you better stay at the window and keep watch for Edward."

"All right. But hurry. And be careful," I added for no good reason I could think of. Except that I remembered the dread I had felt when Robby went to explore the back rooms of the apartment by himself. For a moment or two then I had been assaulted with the idiotic notion that Sally Wright's body was lying in one of those back rooms. But that was ridiculous, wasn't it? It was horrible enough that her own father had been murdered this evening. Surely no further tragedy could befall the family. That only happens in lurid melodramas, in preposterous mystery novels, in the final scene of *Hamlet*, and (a recollection from thirteen months ago vividly appeared in my inner mind and caused me to shudder) that only happens in idyllic little towns like Brookfield. Or Havenport?

"Be careful, Sophie," I called out once again. But there had been no need. She had just returned to the living room with what I could only call "a gloat in her eye." My mind instantly wandered (as it often does when I'm subjected to undue stress) to the delightful Thornton Wilder short story in which this pungent phrase occurs until Sophie interrupted my inner musings with "I was right, boss. Look what I found under Sally's bed."

My distracted mind girded itself for Sophie alluding to the ghastly sight of the young woman's decapitated body. Luckily, it was only a few shards of cracked glass which Sophie held in the palm of her open hand. "These must have fallen under the bed when the cell phone's screen was smashed," she said.

Before I could ask her what this revelation had to do with the missing Sally's whereabouts, Sophie pointed to the window. "Look, Edward's leaving." I turned back and saw that Edward was walking as quickly as he could manage across the lawn and towards the street when he disappeared from our sight. I used the phrase "as quickly as he could manage" because he was carrying something over his shoulder. Something wrapped in what looked like a large piece of tarpaulin. Something that seemed to be very heavy and very bulky.

"My God," I exclaimed, "what is that kid doing?"

"We've got to follow him and find out." Sophie's simple statement caused a chill to descend down my spine. "Follow him? Shouldn't we call Robby?" I sensibly asked.

"I don't think so, Harry. First of all, we have no idea where Edward is headed. By the time Robby got here, he might be difficult or impossible to find. And he might no longer be in possession of whatever it is he's carrying. Secondly and more importantly, Madge is our friend and so is Edward. We owe it to them to be very, very certain of the facts before we rush to any judgments that might damage their lives. If we find that something illegal is indeed going on, we can always call the police then."

I believe I had one or two very viable points to make to refute the logic of Sophie's rather specious argument and would have spoken them I am sure most cogently and calmly had not the phone in the living room then rung. It scared the hell out of both of us. Sophie rushed and answered it on the second ring. It was Barbara Wright calling from the state capital.

"Oh, yes, Barbara, how are you doing? Yes, it's Sophie. Yes, I'm still here. What? It's hard to hear you. Your phone must be breaking up. Are you using a cell phone? Why don't you find a location that has a stronger signal and call me right back. Sally? Um, I can hardly hear you. Call me right back, okay?"

My heart went out to Sophie. She is the most truthful person I have ever met and her attempts to be evasive to Barbara were painful to watch. As soon as Barbara hung up, Sophie reached into her tote bag and pulled out a penlight. "Harry, use this while you follow Edward, and be very careful he doesn't spot you. I'll deal with Barbara somehow. Call me when you discover something. Go on, go, go. You'll lose him." And I was out the door penlight in hand as the phone rang once again in the apartment. I quickly descended the stairs and walked as softly as I could in the direction I had seen Edward take.

No one was around. Of course, it was after midnight, and the village of Havenport always went to bed early. So, the fact that no one was around made perfect sense. Still, hearing only the sound of my own footsteps as I walked down the street prompted one or two sets of very large goose bumps to appear on several rather intimate portions of my anatomy. I felt a chill and felt more than a touch of regret for so hurriedly and perhaps foolhardily leaving the safety and security of the apartment and the companionship of my dear Sophie to enter this darkness, this stillness, this world of night.

I was alone, alone in this silent emptiness with only the small flashlight to show me what was a foot or two ahead of me, not knowing what I would encounter, whom I would encounter. The pounding of my heart was competing with the hollow sound of my footsteps. And then, suddenly, there was a sound far to my right. The unearthly stillness of the night was broken by a sound. It was a sort of faint panting. I immediately thought of my friend Charlie's devoted dog Lucy. And then I thought of the horrors she had encountered in Brookfield. And then more goose bumps appeared, and then I heard the sound again. It came from a human throat. It was faint and quite a distance away, but I definitely heard it, and I did my best to follow it.

I was walking on the shoreline now headed toward the ocean. It must have been very low tide as I could hear the waves only very faintly way in the distance. But I could hear the panting. No, it was more heavy breathing than panting, and it was now accompanied by another sound repeated and repeated again. It was the sound of some heavy bit of machinery or implement hitting the ground. I still could not see anything more than a few feet in front of me, as the moon was hidden by dark, menacing clouds. I couldn't see anything, but suddenly all my faculties were centered in my ears. I followed the sounds unerringly, and all at once the crescent moon emerged from the shrouds that had engulfed it. And I saw a figure in the distance. And he was grunting and perhaps weeping a little. And it was Edward. And the bulky canvas package lay on the ground beside him. And he was lifting what looked like a metal shovel. And he was digging. He was digging a large hole in the ground. Oh, my God. He was digging a grave.

CHAPTER 8

MY HEAD BEGAN TO THROB. I hadn't felt such pain in the last thirteen months. Not since Brookfield. But here it was again. And it was worse than it had ever been. And as my fingers squeezed my right temple fruitlessly trying to stifle the headache, for a moment I heard once again the bullet from the rifle echoing and re-echoing. Once again I saw the blood blossom from Tom Wright's chest. Once again I saw the figure standing atop the cliff holding the rifle, and for the first time I remembered that the tilt of his head seemed to indicate that he was laughing. For the first time I remembered that what I could see of his body type and height looked quite similar to Edward's. I called out his name, and the actual Edward stopped his digging and turned to face me, and I heard a gasping sound that might have come from me, and then there was nothing. Nothing.

Until my father said to me, "So, Harrison, what do you think about fishing?" And I told him I loved it. But I was lying. I hated it. I hated how unsettled the rocking of the flimsy little craft made my stomach feel. I hated how far away from shore we had traveled. I hated the smell of fish that seemed to permeate every inch of the boat. I hated everything about it. But I had insisted. I had made such a big thing about our going out in the rowboat to catch "the big one" that I had to pretend that I was enjoying myself. My father was exerting himself so much that I had to make sure he believed that it was worth all the effort, that I was having the time of my life, that I was loving every moment of the birthday present he had finally agreed to give me and about which I had talked incessantly, bragged for months to all my friends. I was actually going to spend a whole day with my father doing what he enjoyed most, sharing the innermost secrets of his favorite pastime with him. Just the two of us alone in a rowboat determined to catch "the big one." It was going to be such fun, such an adventure. And now that it was actually, finally taking place, I hated it.

But I put on a happy, smiling face. I pretended that I was thrilled that we only had fifteen or twenty minutes more to go before we arrived at that special spot, "my secret place, Harrison, where we might just catch that big one we've always wanted." I pretended that I didn't see how tired he was growing strenuously pushing the oars forward and back, forward and back, struggling against the waves that were no longer gentle, the current that was no longer our friend. I pretended that I didn't notice how strongly the wind had picked up. I nonchalantly held on to the brim of my Mickey Mouse Club cap to prevent it from blowing away. I pretended that I didn't notice the look of concern, of fear perhaps, on his face as we both heard that sharp, splintering sound. I pretended I didn't feel the salt water that splashed against my sneakers.

My right sock was getting really wet. I reached down to roll it up, and I realized I was not in the rowboat with my dad but instead was lying on my side on the soggy ground and that the tide had returned and was lapping at my leg. My pants, shoe and sock were more than damp. I scooted back a few feet, and tried to look around me. But it had grown even darker. The moon had retreated once more behind the ominous clouds. I tried to stand up, but the pain in my head was returning, and it took two or three tries before I could manage that. I looked in Edward's direction. But from what I could see he was no longer there. I was alone, and there was a throbbing pain in my head, and I was wet, and, even more importantly, it dawned on me that I was scared. Really scared.

As I massaged my aching temple, I tried to find the penlight Sophie had given me. I must have dropped it when I passed out. But try as I might, I could not locate the damned thing. I *was* able to retrieve my cell phone from my pocket. Luckily, its front screen had not been smashed as had Sally's. I turned on the phone, and as I waited for it to come to life I thought about Sally and her father and Edward and the predicament in which I now found myself.

What was I doing here? Alone, in the dark, on a narrow stretch of sodden earth, wet, cold, miserable. Here I was—a successful man of the theatre, a highly regarded celebrity, a Tony award nominee for heaven's sake—traipsing around in the dead of night (and I use that term not at all lightly), and for what reason? To catch a possible murderer in the act of burying his latest victim? Possibly a double murderer? Possibly a serial killer who possibly tried to murder me or Sophie before or after he possibly murdered a young, innocent co-ed, the owner or former owner of a smashed bright-pink, faux diamond-encrusted cellular phone?

What was I doing here? Sophie had convinced me that I needed a well-deserved rest. Some rest! Robby had strongly suggested that Sophie and I hightail it out of this picturesque picture postcard of a village, this Kodak—winning photo stop as fast as we could. As my mind continued to race wildly, I now was convinced that

Robby was absolutely correct. We should and would leave this faux diamond-encrusted deathtrap immediately. That is, if I ever managed to find my way out of this dank darkness and back to civilization and Sophie, and that seemed to be incumbent on getting this wretched phone to work and calling for help. But so far there was no success to report on that front. As the maddening phrase "Searching for Network" tauntingly remained on the face of the phone, I slowly forced myself to walk towards where I had last seen Edward. The minimal illumination from the phone's back lighted screen was all I had to guide my way. I reached what I thought was the approximate location but could find nothing to indicate that there had been recent activity there.

Had I imagined it? Had I passed out and then imagined that I had seen Edward digging what looked like a grave as I had imagined I was back with my father in that cursed rowboat? And why had I passed out or collapsed or fainted or whatever had happened to me? What had caused that? Was there something seriously wrong with me? Was I losing my mind?

By holding the cell phone next to my watch, I could barely make out that it was now almost one in the morning. How long had I been unconscious? Had there been enough time for Edward to conclude whatever it was he had been doing and cover up the hole he had dug? And then where had he gone? Had he indeed been the rifleman on the cliff? Had Tom Wright been the intended victim? Or had I? Or Sophie? Was Edward the mysterious person who had been stalking Sophie? Had Edward murdered Sally after she told him he was coming on too strong? A thousand more questions flooded my overheated brain as the headache pulsed even more rapidly and forcefully.

No! No more questions. I no longer cared what was going on. This was none of my business. This was none of my concern. I was getting the hell away from *happy little Havenport*. And Sophie was going with me.

Apparently the wretched phone would never snag a signal from this spot. So I turned to my left and walked away from the encroaching tide. It was hard going with only the cell phone's light to see by, but I only managed to stumble two or three times before I noticed that I was climbing up a gradual incline and within a few minutes reached the road that encircled the shoreline. There was nothing, no one in sight. I turned and slowly began trudging in what I hoped was the direction from which I had started. I could not tell where exactly I had emerged or how far I was from the general store. And Sophie. And safety. And Mrs. Donohue's warm and comforting hot toddies and . . .

The blaring sound of the Fifth Brandenburg Concerto scared the bejeezus out of me as my cell phone finally sprang to life. I pressed the Talk button and merely said, "Hello." I was rather surprised how raspy and exhausted my voice sounded.

Sophie seemed surprised too. "My God, Harry, you sound like hell. How are you? Where are you? I've been going out of my mind with worry. What's happened?"

"Which of your innumerable and rather tedious questions, my dear Sophie, would you like me to answer first?" I responded in an attempt to appear as near to my normal self as I could.

It seemed to have worked as Sophie breathed a very audible sigh of relief. "Well, at least you're alive. And as cranky as usual. Where are you? Madge and I are in her car on the sea road."

"You're with Madge?"

"Yes, and we've been worried sick."

"I'm not quite sure exactly where, but I am on the sea road as well headed eastward I believe. I'm not quite sure how far . . ."

"Oh, Harry, I think I see you. I can barely see a faint light moving towards us. I think it's from your phone."

Sophie had indeed spotted me, and in three or four minutes I was in the back seat of Madge's life-saving chariot out of the darkness, out of danger for the moment at least, no longer alone. After hugging me harder than I had ever been hugged before, Sophie sat next to me in the parked car, while Madge worriedly looked back at us from the driver's seat and asked me, "Did you find Edward?"

I didn't know what to say. How much had Sophie told Madge? I gave Sophie an imploring look to which she replied, "It's all right, Harry. I told Madge everything that happened tonight. She asked me for the truth. So I gave it to her. I told her about the broken cell phone that Robby found in Sally's bedroom. I told her that we had seen Edward carry something heavy wrapped in canvas from the storage shed and that you tried to follow him."

"Did you see where he went, Harry? Did you find Edward?" Madge's voice was strained and her eyes red from weeping as she repeated her question to me. My heart went out to her.

"I think I did, Madge. But I'm not totally positive. I collapsed about the time that I thought I saw Edward, so I'm not sure I really did see him and whether or not he was really digging that hole. It was dark, and he was a distance from me, and my head was splitting . . ."

"Digging a hole?" Madge could barely get out the words.

"Yes, with a shovel. A large hole."

"My God, Harry." Sophie's voice was as full of expression as was Madge's.

"Madge," I then asked, "Why did you drive back to see Sophie?"

She was still for a moment trying to absorb what I had told her. Then she said quietly and sadly, "After we had gone back to the house, Edward said he didn't want to talk anymore. So he went immediately to his room. I decided to make him a cup of hot cocoa. He's always loved that since he was a little boy. With a dollop of Marshmallow Fluff on top. I prepared it and brought it upstairs. There was no answer to my knock or when I softly called his name. I supposed he must have dropped off as soon as he had gotten into bed. I tiptoed into the room to leave the cocoa on his bedside table in case he woke up later. And that's when I found the note.

"Note?" I asked.

Madge handed me the folded piece of paper. "The bedroom window was wide open. He was gone, and this was addressed to me."

It was so dark in the car that Sophie switched on the overhead light. The handwriting was a little difficult to decipher. The note had obviously been written in a hurry.

Mom,

Please forgive me. I have to go away for awhile. I'll let you know where I am soon. I've got a lot to think about, to understand. Maybe Mr. Hunt can help explain what happened. Please don't think badly of me. I love you very much.

It was signed *Eddie*.

"He hasn't used that name since he was eight years old," Madge whispered. "He only called himself that when he was sorry. Sorry for doing something bad."

Chapter 9

"Since you and Sophie hadn't returned to the house," Madge continued, "I drove back to the Wrights' apartment to show you the note and find out if you could help provide an explanation for any of this. Edward seemed to think you might be able to do that. Can you? Can you, Harry?" Madge was talking so low now that I could barely hear her. The look in her eyes though said everything. She wanted, no, *desperately needed* me to offer words of solace. She needed me to tell her everything would be all right, that we would most certainly get to the bottom of this mess, and that all would turn out happily ever after for her son, for her, for Sally, for everyone. Madge needed hope.

But could I give it to her? After all I had gone through this wretched evening (perhaps the worst of my life), I had reached the decision that I would follow Robby's sensible, rational advice: Sophie and I would get the hell out of here and fast.

I wanted to tell Madge Magill that although I wished the very best for Edward, for her, for everyone, there was nothing I could do to help. I had no explanation whatsoever for the sudden disappearance of Sally, for Edward's strange behavior this evening, for the murder of Tom Wright, or for anything else that in the last eight hours or so had transformed this peaceful little fishing village into a frightening, chaotic conundrum. A conundrum I not only could not explain but had no desire to do so.

I was searching my brain for the kindest, most supportive way I could think of to tell all this to Madge when Sophie beat me to it. And what she said was indeed kind and supportive and made me want to administer to her "Necessity's sharp pinch!" on the body part where it would smart the most.

What she said was, "Of course, we'll help, Madge. We may not have the solution yet for all that's happened. In fact, I think we're both as much in the dark as you are. But I guarantee you that the boss and I will do everything in our power to find out what's going on and help Edward. We promise you that, Madge. Don't we, Harry?"

And now *both* Madge and Sophie were looking at me with big soulful eyes, full of hope and anticipation. They were both looking forward to my expected expression of solidarity with their cause, optimism about our chances of success, reassurance that all would soon be hunky-dory in Havenport.

Well, sorry to disappoint you, girls. I was not about to change my well-thought-out, remarkably logical and commonsensical decision. I was resolute. I was steadfast. I was full of it. So, after one more look into their trusting eyes, I of course crumbled and said, "We'll do our best, Madge."

To which she of course replied, "That's all I could ask for, Harry. Thank you." She wiped a tear away, and, I blush to admit, so did I.

"Well, if we're going to accomplish anything worthwhile, I suggest we start immediately," Sophie interjected. "I would think our first order of business is finding Edward. Let's stop him if we can before he manages to leave . . ."

"The scene of the crime?" Madge filled in Sophie's verbal ellipsis for her. Neither Sophie nor I knew where to look. "Listen, Harry and Sophie, I am fully aware that Edward seems to be implicated in some really serious business. So there's no need to pussyfoot around my feelings. Do you agree?"

We both nodded our assent. I remembered why I liked Madge so much. I then asked her, "Do you have any idea where Edward might have gone?"

"Well, Harry," she responded, "as much as I hate to admit it, Edward might have decided to go see his father. That has often been his pattern when he needed to get away from me for a bit after we had a little spat or after he found himself in some particular little difficulty at home. I always considered it rather a slap in the face. Right or wrong, he knew that his father would always take his side. Only of course so the bum could always make the situation just a little more difficult for me. Quite a sweetheart that man is."

"But Ethan lives on the west coast, doesn't he?" Sophie asked.

"Yes, he does. In Washington state to be exact. Way out in the boondocks. Where a man could be a man—as he incessantly loved to put it—and hunt and fish and scratch himself to his heart's content."

"How long have you been divorced?" I asked needing my memory refreshed.

"Since Edward was ten. You remember him, don't you Sophie?"

"Oh, yes. When he was still the whiz kid of Wall Street."

"Right. Before he cashed in his load of chips and left everything and everyone for the backwoods and freedom."

"How often did Edward see his father?" I asked.

"He spent major holidays there as well as his spring and winter breaks. Plus the occasional visit to join his father on a special camping or hunting trip. He spent the summers with me and my folks here in Havenport."

"So, if Edward wants to go to his father, how does he do it at one o'clock in the morning? In fact, I'm not sure how he managed to get back to the general store so quickly. You only have one car, and you drove it over here."

"That's right, Harry. Edward rode his bicycle. When I found out Edward had sneaked out of his room, I went to the garage and saw that his bike was missing."

"Let's get the chronology straight," I said assuming the air of a military tactician. I noticed that Sophie was writing down what I was saying in the notebook she produced from her tote bag. "Edward biked back to the Wrights' place, hid behind a tree till he saw Robby drive off, opened the storage shed, removed something from it and carried it to the beach where, unless I totally hallucinated the whole thing, he began to dig a hole presumably to bury it. That's when I collapsed like an idiot." I paused for an instant to allow the ladies to refute the disparaging term I had applied to myself. A little miffed when they didn't, I continued. "When I woke up, I found that Edward had gone. In a cursory search, I could find no trace of the hole. Had he enough time to finish what he was doing and cover it all up?"

"You were gone about an hour, Harry," Sophie said. "Edward probably had enough time to, to . . ."

"To bury Sally's body," Madge once again verbalized what Sophie and I had been thinking. "I know how bad this looks for Edward," Madge went on. "But I know my son. He could not be a murderer. However, whether he is or not, I want the truth to come out. And to discover the truth, we need to find Edward."

"I presume he left the bike somewhere near the general store. Do you think he went back there to retrieve it?"

"Madge and I did take a few moments to try to locate the bike near the store before we got into her car to search for you," Sophie said. "We didn't see any trace of it."

"Let's assume then that after Edward left the beach he went back to his bicycle and then rode off somewhere. His goal might have been to get to Washington State somehow. Probably as quickly as possible. What would he have done then? Where would he have gone? Any ideas?"

"Well, Harry," Madge said, "as you know, the nearest airport is at the state capital, and that's about forty miles away."

I stated the obvious, "I'm sure he didn't decide to ride his bike there."

"No," Madge continued. "There are only two possible ways I can think of that he could get there without having his own car: Noah Benson's livery service or the ferry. And the last ferry to town leaves at 9:00 p.m."

I had first met Noah Benson when Madge had arranged for him to pick us up in his limo at the railroad station ten days ago and drive us to Havenport. He also owned several medium sized boats which he hired out for fishing expeditions and sightseeing. Both he and his wife were proud members of the Little Players, and I had given them several notes at rehearsals which they had taken quite seriously like the one this afternoon about Emilia's use of "thou" in *Othello*. The Bensons impressed me as hard-working, decent and perfectly pleasant residents of the village. The salt of the earth. Madge started the car, and within a few minutes we were nearing the Benson home near the wharf. "It's so late," I said. "I'd hate to wake them up if we're mistaken."

Sophie responded by saying, "The lights in the house are on. They must be up. And look, there's a bike parked outside."

Madge was the first one out of the car and had already rung the doorbell by the time Sophie and I joined her on the front porch. The middle-aged Mrs. Benson, clad in a long bathrobe that revealed only the top of her sensible nightgown, answered the door on the second ring.

"I'm sorry to disturb you so early in the morning, Nora, but it's very important."

"That's perfectly all right, Mrs. Magill, I was up already. I would think it's about Edward. Am I right?"

"Yes, yes you are," I blurted out.

"Oh, hello, Mr. Hunt and Miss Sophie too. How are you folks doing?"

"We're rather worried about Edward, Mrs. Benson."

"Yes, and so am I," Nora Benson added with a worried expression on her face.

She told us that her husband had received a call from Edward about two hours ago asking to be driven to the airport. He said that if was a family emergency and that he had to get on a plane as soon as possible. When Mr. Benson had told him that he doubted any planes would be taking off until the morning, Edward replied that he would wait at the airport in order to get the first available flight out of there. "He said that you were too upset, Mrs. Magill, to drive him there yourself."

"Well, yes, Nora, I am upset, but not because of a family emergency. At least not in the way my son made it sound."

Mrs. Benson then told us that Edward had arrived at their house about forty or forty-five minutes ago. "Looking at him, Noah was a little reluctant to take him to the airport."

"Why was that?" I asked.

"Well . . ." Mrs. Benson hesitated a bit and then said, "I'm afraid it was pretty obvious that Edward had been drinking. Quite a bit. He even asked Noah for a drink. But of course he told him we didn't have anything in the house."

"But your husband did take him?"

"Yes, Mr. Hunt, he did I'm afraid. They left about, oh, thirty-five minutes ago I would think," she said looking at the kitchen clock. It was one of those cutesy old-fashioned black and white Felix-the-Cat-looking wall clocks. I had seen a number of them decorating kitchens in Havenport. For some reason, I couldn't help staring at the cat's moving eyes and tail while I collected my thoughts.

Sophie was still right on target as she asked, "Did Edward say where he wanted to go or what airline he planned to take?"

"I'm afraid not that I heard."

Sophie continued, "Would it be possible for you to call your husband now so that his mother could speak to Edward?"

"I would be happy to do that, but when he and Edward left, Noah somehow forgot to take his cell phone. See it's right here on the counter. I'm so sorry. Would you folks like a cup of hot tea or something? It won't take but a minute."

"Thank you, no, Nora. We're in a hurry. Thank you for your time."

"No problem. No problem at all, Mrs. Magill. I hope you catch him. Good luck."

Mrs. Benson's last words were addressed to thin air, since the three of us were already out the door. Madge started the car, and we were off.

Chapter 10

I sat next to Madge. Sophie was in the back seat busily updating her notes to include our conversation with Nora Benson. Madge was driving, or perhaps I should say Madge was driving like a crazy person. I knew from the several excursions we had taken with Madge since our arrival in Havenport that she was an excellent driver. I tried to remind myself of that as the car rounded the winding curves of the cliff-lined road at speeds that made my heart beat faster than normal. In fact, many of my internal organs were working overtime, especially my stomach. Although Sophie and I had not eaten since our early supper, (When was that, five or six hundred years ago?) I could now identify and re-taste every ingredient of that light repast as we took a particularly hazardous turn. I wanted to ask Madge if she thought she might be going a little too fast on this dangerous road, but looking at the determined expression on her face and the way her hands grasped the steering wheel in a death grip (Just a colorful expression, I hoped.) I decided against it.

Instead, I turned back to look at Sophie and asked her how she had handled her phone conversation with Barbara Wright.

"Well, Harry," Sophie told me, "Barbara was in a pretty bad state when she called the second time. She was certain that Sally must have taken the news of her father's death badly. That was the only explanation Barbara could think of for Sally's failure to call her back. I then had to tell her that Sally hadn't returned home yet. She became so upset that I had to spill what Edward had said. I told her he hadn't driven Sally home. Instead, she had called one of her girl friends for a ride. Barbara then surmised that Sally must have stayed overnight at the friend's house."

Although she didn't say so, I felt assured that Sophie hadn't told Barbara about Sally's shattered cell phone or Edward's visit to the storage shed.

Sophie went on, "Barbara asked me the friend's name. When I told her I didn't know, she said she would immediately call the homes of all Sally's friends to find where she was staying and talk to Sally herself. I proposed, since it was now so late and she must be so emotionally drained, it might be wiser for her to postpone making those calls until the morning. She was calling from the hospital where Tom's body had been taken. A doctor had offered her a room there and had suggested giving her something to help her sleep. I told her that was an excellent idea. She would be in a better state to talk to her daughter after a good night's rest. She eventually agreed and said she would call me after she spoke to Sally in the morning. She would also have a better idea then when the police would be finished with their tests and she could make the necessary arrangements for the funeral. I feel so badly for her. First the shock of her husband's death and then this uncertainty about Sally."

"I feel for her too, Sophie. It's excruciating not knowing where your child is or what's happening to him." The heartache Madge was feeling as she said these words was so apparent that I instinctively put my hand on hers as it clutched the steering wheel. Suddenly, my hand was hurled off as Madge frantically turned the wheel to avoid hitting an eighteen-wheeler that had appeared out of nowhere in the darkness and was rapidly approaching us having strayed too far into our lane. The blaring sound of the truck's horn and its blinding headlights shocked all of us. It missed us only by inches, and as we heard it roaring away in the distance, Madge pulled over onto the gravel edge of the road and stopped the car. She was shaking. I was too. "I don't think I can drive any more now," she said. There was no missing the trace of hysteria in her voice.

Sophie immediately sprang into action. "No problem, Madge. I'll take over." She opened the back door and climbed out.

"But you don't know the roads the way I do."

"Never fear. With you beside me as navigator, we gals will do just fine piloting this buggy of yours. The two of us will make Germaine Greer proud." The way Sophie said this while doing a few impromptu knee bends was so ridiculous that we all had to laugh. "Get a move on there, Harry. We've got an airport to reach."

"Aye, aye, captain," I saluted as I scooted into the back seat. As the car started up again with its new redoubtable driver very much in command, I thought how grateful I was that Sophie was in my life. It was not the first time I had thought that.

I was also glad Sophie had assumed the role of driver. I was not at all sure that I would have been able to do so. It had been thirteen months since I had driven a car. The image of the two vehicles colliding with such force and the terrible sound of that high-pitched scream were *the stuff that my dreams were made on* (or, rather, my nightmares) for many months after we had left Brookfield.

And there was no reason for me to get behind the wheel at all. Living and working in Manhattan, I had no need for a car, and when I was booked to deliver lectures throughout the country a limousine and driver always met us at the airport and were always at our disposal.

My reluctance to drive was why we had chosen to take the train to Havenport. And it had worked out very well. The village was so small that there had not been any need for either of us to drive. Walking or bike riding had more than adequately sufficed. And, on the few occasions when we had wanted to travel some distance from Havenport, Madge had been delighted to play the chauffeur. So, no driving for me, at least for the immediate future, thank you very much.

As the miles ticked away on the odometer, every fifteen minutes or so Madge tried to reach Edward on his cell phone. She had done this so often since she had discovered him missing that it had become almost a silent ritual for her to perform. And always the result was the same: "Hi, there. This is Edward. I can't come to the phone right now, but leave a message and I'll get back to you right away. Have a good day." It had not been a good day for poor Madge.

As we got closer and closer to the airport, I leaned back and tried to prepare myself for whatever we would encounter there. I slowly became aware that the throbbing in my right temple had abated, but still my head ached. Strangely, it was the back of my head that now was causing me pain. I reached back, and the pressure of my index finger caused me to yelp. There was a large bump or bruise there, and it hurt like hell. Sophie heard the sound that I had made and asked me what was wrong. I told her I must have bumped my head on the ground when I had passed out and asked her for an aspirin or two. She told me to look in her tote bag which was in the back seat next to me. From that ever-ready indispensable treasure trove I pulled out a small bottle of aspirins. I swallowed four tablets and washed them down with a swig from the water bottle I also found there. Sophie said she'd take a look at "that thick skull of yours" as soon as we reached our destination.

It was a little after two o'clock in the morning when we finally pulled into the nearly deserted airport parking lot. Once again, Madge was first out of the car. Sophie and I really had to move to catch up with her. I looked for Noah's limousine in the lot but didn't see it. Could we have somehow arrived at the airport before him, despite his half hour head start? Or had he already dropped Edward off and left? We would soon know for sure. The sound of our footsteps crossing the lot brought back scary memories of a similar early morning visit to a deserted airport in Brookfield. But this airport was just outside the state capital and, though not gigantic, was considerably larger than the other.

There were only a few people about the main concourse of the sole terminal. They appeared to be homeless. But no sign of Edward. We saw the arrival and departure board and headed for it. Just as Mr. Benson had told Edward, no flight was scheduled to take off until six o'clock, and that was a flight to LaGuardia. We found the ticket counter for that airline, but there was no one on duty. There was though a telephone on the counter. The small sign next to it advised to "Dial 1 for Assistance." Madge reached for it, and while she waited for a response Sophie and I signaled to her that we would look around some more and be back in a few minutes.

Where could he be? Was he here at all? My eyes scanned the concourse. There was a small restaurant or luncheonette in one corner. There were rest rooms, a few telephone booths and two vending machines located in another. Opposite the rest rooms was a stairway leading upwards. There were several unmarked doors near the stairs. And that seemed to be all there was.

As we walked the hundred yards or so to the rest rooms, I probed once more the bump on the back of my head. The salutary effect of the aspirins was waning, and the pain was returning. Examining my hand, I saw there were flecks of dried blood on my index finger. But we had reached the bathrooms. I would deal with my injury later.

Checking that the phone booths were empty, Sophie went into the Ladies' Room. "Just to cover all bases," she said. I entered the Men's. No one was there that I could see. But just to make sure, I decided to look in each of the three stalls even though I saw no tell-tale feet. The first was empty. The second was . . . "Oh, I'm so sorry," I said to the tiny old man with the shaggy beard and dirty overcoat who was sitting on the commode with the door unlocked reading a copy of what could possibly have been *The New Yorker*. I didn't stay long enough to check out his choice of reading material any further. Closing his door and pushing open the door of the final stall (noting to my relief that it was unoccupied), I exited the room in a hurry almost running into Sophie outside. "No one in mine," she said. "No one we know in mine," I countered breathing rather heavily. Giving me an odd look, she followed me as I crossed the concourse and reached the front of the small restaurant.

"I doubt if it would be open yet," Sophie said. I tended to agree with her. The front window was so heavily covered with notices of their daily specials that I couldn't see much inside. But there did appear to be a light on. Probably only for security reasons I surmised. However, I tried the door just in case and was surprised when it opened. "Well, what do you know?" Sophie said under her breath before following me in.

Cousin Carrie's Home Style Cooking was an unusually attractive little eatery for an airport of any size. "The flowery chintz fabrics blend surprisingly well with the New England maritime motifs producing an atmosphere of welcoming cozy comfort," I said. No, I hadn't just composed this rhapsodic review of the restaurant's décor out of thin air. Rather, I read it aloud to Sophie from the framed poster-size reprint of a month-old Zagat-like rave prominently placed near the front door.

"Indeed," Sophie responded.

Yet despite its acclaim, the place was empty. No one was seated in any of Cousin Carrie's comfortable-looking booths or at the attractive bleached-pine counter. So why was the door unlocked, and why were the lights on? I was just about to ask Sophie this when we heard a sound coming from what I assumed was the kitchen. We held our breaths and listened as intently as we could. The sound we heard was a dull thud accompanied by a muffled human voice. The thud sounded once, twice more. We tiptoed as quietly as we could till we were standing next to the closed kitchen door. We heard the voice once again. Though it was difficult to decipher, I think I heard something that sounded very much like: "Help."

I slammed the door open and saw . . . nothing. At least at first. Then we heard the muffled voice again. It seemed to be coming from behind the large wooden work table. We rushed behind it and found to our astonishment an old woman with a dish towel stuffed in her mouth. Her hands were tied behind her back with what looked like her apron strings. She was lying on the floor with her shoes up against the table. The thumps we heard must have been caused by her kicking the table trying to get our attention.

I expected words of gratitude to come out of the poor woman's mouth as I removed her gag. Instead, a string of expletives flooded out, many of which I hadn't heard in years if ever. She was using language, as Alan Jay Lerner aptly put it, "that would make a sailor blush." When she finally took a slight breath, she looked at me and said accusingly,

"Well, don't just sit there. Get him! Get that young bastard! He just ran out. Don't let him get away!"

"Where did he go?" I asked bewilderedly.

"Out the back door, you imbecile," she screamed.

We ran out the open back door of the kitchen and found ourselves in a service corridor. We followed it till we were back in the concourse. I desperately searched the space with my eyes. I could see no one in the least suspicious. Two obviously tired cleaning women with scarves tied around their heads pushing a mop and a pail of water on wheels, respectively, were heading for the service corridor.

"Did you see anyone running through here just now?" I almost screamed at them. "A young man about twenty-one? About six feet, thin, dark hair?"

I must have appeared like a madman to them. But the older woman did say, "Somebody like that just went up there." She pointed to the staircase across the concourse.

Without taking the time to thank her, I told Sophie to go back and stay with the restaurant owner as I ran across the concourse and saw Madge beginning to climb the stairs. "Harry, I think I just saw Edward go up here." I rushed past her after reading the sign with an arrow pointing upwards standing next to the staircase. The sign read: "To the Observation Platform."

I sprinted up the stairs faster than I ever thought I could. I started to lose my breath as I reached the third and final landing. There was a closed door in front of me. I pushed it open and climbed up onto the top of a tower about sixty feet off the ground. There were several small coin-operated telescopes stationed around the half wall that circled the platform. I looked in front of me. No one was there. I heard the door behind me open and heard Madge call my name as she climbed out. I turned to help her, and that's when I saw Edward standing there.

At the back of the platform. He looked crazed as he climbed atop the waist-high protective wall and stood there on the edge for a second. Then he called out, "Sally. Don't worry. I'll join you." Madge screamed when she saw her son jump off the tower.

Chapter 11

It was indeed a miracle that he had not immediately died from the fall. The paramedics had said that to his mother, and she had repeated it to us while they performed their life-saving emergency procedures. She repeated it again and again until it became a sort of mantra that seemed to help keep not only Edward but Madge herself alive.

"It's a miracle that he's alive," she said to us as the medics connected the shattered and unconscious body to the emergency respirator. "It's God's own miracle," she said to us as she held her son's hand before he was lifted on the gurney into the ambulance. It was his left hand that she held and then kissed.

Trying like the devil to avoid looking into Madge's eyes and the torment I knew they would reveal, I looked away and focused on that left hand and concentrated my attention on that odd crescent-shaped birthmark of his I had noticed four or five hours ago. Anything not to look into Madge's eyes. But I couldn't avoid hearing her voice and the request that she soon made, the first of several I would receive in the next few hours.

"It's God's miracle that he's alive, and—the mantra now changed substantially—it's God's will that you, Harrison Hunt, are here. In his own words my son asked for your help. And it's God's will, God's plan that you are here to grant his plea. It's God's plan that you, Harrison Hunt, will find out what really happened here tonight, what really happened to Edward. You will clear Edward's name and reputation by discovering the truth, and the truth shall set us all free. It's God's will, God's plan. You won't forsake God's plan, will you Harry? No, of course you won't, you're God's deputy now, Harry. And you will start right now."

"First, we'll follow you to the hospital in the car, "Sophie said as Madge climbed into the ambulance next to Edward.

"No," Madge turned to us. "There's nothing for you to do at the hospital. Don't waste a minute. You'll take my car and stay at my house while I care for my son, and you will discover the truth." She looked directly at me as she said, "Find the truth, Harry. Help Edward. Find the truth, please." Then she asked, "Did you know it's a miracle that my son is still living?" The last question was delivered with a smile to the E.M.T. person Madge sat beside as the door to the ambulance was closed and, sirens wailing, it receded from the airport into the distance.

When she had made that request of me, I had finally been forced to look directly into Madge's eyes and was surprised by what I saw there. Not anguish, not desperation but, rather, hope, faith, and (Could it be?) a trace of serenity.

Sophie and I stood in the airport parking lot listening to the fading sirens until we could hear them no longer. And then Sophie turned to me and said, "So you're God's deputy now, are you?"

"Who wouldda thunk it?" I replied. But there was no laughter in my voice, no sparkle in my eye. Why? Because I was terrified, that's why. Terrified of the responsibility that had been thrust upon me, and terrified of failing. How could I ever face Madge again if I could not do what she had asked? And was there any way of succeeding at all? What if the truth I discovered was that Edward had killed Sally and buried her corpse? What if he also had been the man who had shot at us in the boat and had killed Tom? (From what I remembered he certainly matched the rifleman physically.) If Edward hadn't been plagued by guilt over these actions, why then had he written that note to his mother, why had he run away, why had be been heavily drinking, why had he gone to the airport to escape, why had he gagged and tied up that woman in the restaurant, and why had he finally attempted suicide crying out that he would soon join Sally in the afterlife? Multiple questions that Madge insisted I answer with a plausible explanation that would clear her son of all wrongdoings. No wonder I was terrified.

And I believe Sophie saw all that I was feeling in one probing look. And she responded by giving my arm a tender squeeze and repeating quietly to me what she had said a while ago to Madge, "All we can do is try our best." Have I mentioned how fortunate I was to have Sophie in my life?

"I only hope that our best will be good enough," I sighed. "All right, so what do we do first?"

"I think the first order of business is for both of us to go back to the house and get some much needed sleep. We'll then be able to think much more clearly." Sophie's suggestion was sensible as always. But who ever said 'God's deputy' was sensible?

"Sleep will have to wait, I'm afraid, Sophie. Madge wanted us to begin our investigations immediately. So, let's investigate."

As I started walking back into the airport terminal, there was the sound of a car driving out of the parking lot. I didn't look back, but Sophie did. "That's strange," she said. I gave her a questioning look to which she replied, "Out of the corner of my eye I caught a quick glance at the car that just left. It could have been the silver limousine that Noah Benson drives."

"I'm pretty certain it wasn't in the lot when we arrived at the airport," I said. "Do you think he returned and then left again?"

"Who knows?" Sophie looked somewhat bewildered. "I could be wrong. I just got a quick look at it."

Asking Sophie to make a note to question Mr. Benson about this later, we entered the terminal.

There were more people there now, and most of them were police. I nodded at the officer who had questioned Sophie and me earlier while we were waiting for the ambulance to arrive. He nodded back and continued questioning one of the homeless people who had been gathered together and seated in one small area. There were six of them there patiently waiting to give their stories to the police. I noticed my tiny acquaintance from the rest room still reading his magazine. I softly chuckled to myself. It *was The New Yorker*. A few service staff personnel were seated in another section awaiting questioning.

Since the police were all occupied right now, I said to Sophie, "Shall we go back to the restaurant and see if we can get more information from the woman with the salty vocabulary?"

"Might as well," Sophie said. "I didn't get to talk to her much before all hell broke loose when Edward jumped."

We turned in that direction just in time to see the lady in question locking the restaurant's front door. "Wait a second, Mrs. Gillespie. Please wait."

Hearing Sophie call her, she looked at us and with the sourest of expressions sighed dramatically and waited for us to reach her. "Oh, no, not you two idiots again," she addressed us in her typically sweet and polite way. "Haven't I been put through enough torture for one night. What is it you want from me now?"

"Mrs. Gillespie, we weren't able to talk much before. We would be very grateful if you could give us a few minutes of your time."

"And why should I do that, young woman? I told all I knew to the police. I have no intention of wasting the rest of what's left of this god-awful night jabbering with you two lunkheads. Now, out of my way," she exploded as she marched away from us across the concourse and out the front door.

"Well, that went well," I said.

"What a battleaxe," was Sophie's evaluation. "I wrote down what she said to me in the restaurant. She was in such a state that basically all I got were her name, rank and serial number." Taking out her notebook, Sophie recounted that the woman's name was Jessie Gillespie. She was the regional manager for all the Cousin Carrie Home Cooking restaurants in this part of the state. Apparently it was quite a successful restaurant chain. The manager of this one at the airport was out today, so she came by herself to empty the register and settle the day's accounts. The restaurant closed at ten o'clock, but she had been busy at their largest branch until way after midnight and only got here about one forty-five this morning. She had just unlocked the front door when she was pushed inside by a young man who then tied her up in the kitchen and was about to return to the front and empty the register when he heard us enter and bolted out the back door.

"It's pretty late at night for a woman her age to be working, don't you think? How old do you think Mrs. Gillespie is?"

"I would say she's in her late sixties, early seventies, boss. But from what we saw, I would say she's such a feisty old bird that I bet she can handle most anything and is probably pretty darned good at her job. I'm sure she doesn't take any guff from any one."

"It must have been tough for her to be trussed up as she was. She must have been quite embarrassed to have been overcome like that. Maybe that accounts for her behavior to us."

"Maybe, but I think that type of behavior is pretty second nature to her."

"You may be right, Sophie. You may be right. Are we sure that it was Edward who did this to her?"

"It seems conclusive. I asked her what her assailant looked like and she gave me a very detailed description that matched Edward very well. She described the clothes he was wearing pretty much to a tee."

"I suppose it's possible that he needed money to buy the plane ticket and get away, but for him to do it this way seems so unbelievable, so out of character."

"Everything that he's done tonight is so unlike the Edward that I know that I'm completely flummoxed as well, Harry. I've known Edward practically all his life. He's always been such a good kid, smart, serious, thoughtful. He's never been rash or impulsive or vicious. I never, ever would have believed he could steal or rough up anyone, let alone an old lady, or that he could be . . ."

"A murderer," I finished Sophie's thought. "I know what you mean. It's unbelievable. There's no chance he has an evil twin brother, is there?" I said expressing all the frustration I was feeling.

"No chance, Harry. Remember how far your twin theory got you in Brookfield."

"Don't rub it in. All right, so now that we've lost our chance to give poor Mrs. Gillespie the third degree, what's left for us to do here? I feel that I'm failing Madge more and more as each second goes by. Ow!" Without being aware of it, I had scratched the back of my head while talking and saw stars for a moment.

"Your head's still hurting, I see. Why didn't you talk to the paramedics about it when you had the chance? When I suggested it, you nearly bit *my* head off."

"They were too busy trying to keep the boy alive. Don't worry, if it's still bothering me I'll check with a doctor."

"You'd better," Sophie admonished.

"All right, all right, I promise. So what is there left for us to check out around here? How about our giving that service corridor a look-see? I just ran through it in one minute trying to catch up with Edward."

Agreeing with my idea, Sophie walked with me around the corner of the restaurant into the corridor. We walked past the back door of the restaurant after noting that it had been securely locked by the formidable Mrs. Gillespie. There was another door about twenty feet farther along. I opened it, and we entered a large room that appeared to be a general repository for maintenance equipment used at the airport. We noticed a floor waxer, brooms, brushes, mops, pails, and the like. Sophie quickly wrote down in her notebook what we found there. There were two inside doors which led to separate changing and rest room areas for male and female employees. After knocking, we peeked into both. Sophie continued listing what we found in them. Lockers; bins for laundry collection in which were towels, uniforms, scarves and the like; toilets, sinks, and showers were the main features of the two large rooms.

Not finding anything of particular significance, we continued till we reached the end of the corridor. (I chose not to use the phrase "dead end" for obvious reasons.) Placed next to the back wall was a medium-sized dumpster. I cringed knowing Sophie's proclivity for dumpster diving. She did lift the cover, took a few notes and then shaking her head we returned the way we had come, a bit disappointed.

As we passed Cousin Carrie's once again, Sophie made another note for herself. "I think I'll check with the police in a few days to find out if Edward's fingerprints were found in the restaurant," she told me. I thought it was a good idea, but wondered if the police would reveal information like that to us. We would find out in a few days, I imagined.

Back in the concourse, the police appeared to have finished with the six people in the tattered clothing and were now talking to the second small group. The uniforms they wore seemed to indicate they were cleaners or maintenance men. That last word proved to be significant, at least to Sophie.

"Hey, boss," she said. "All the cleaning people sitting over there are men. Where are the two cleaning women we talked to?"

I was perplexed for a moment and then remembered that we had seen two cleaning women crossing the concourse on their way to the service corridor. The older woman had mentioned she had seen a young man go up the staircase to the observation deck.

"Do you think the police finished talking to them already, and they've gone home?" I queried. To answer that question for myself, I went over to the policeman who had talked to us earlier. He had just finished questioning a maintenance man.

When he had first told us his name, it had been hard for me to keep a straight face. I had been so tempted to start singing Sondheim's brilliant lyrics to him.

> We're very upset
>
> We never had the love
>
> That every child oughta get

I was so tempted that I almost got a nose bleed from keeping them buttoned up inside me. But I managed to do so *somehow, someday, somewhere*. I really had to stop doing that. With her eyes rolling, Sophie said she greatly admired my self-restraint when I told her about it.

So now, a smile barely escaped my lips as I said to him, "Officer Krupke, we were wondering where the two cleaning women we saw earlier had gone. At least one of them said she saw someone who looked like Edward."

"I don't believe we talked to any cleaning women, Mr. Hunt. But we should be getting the list of names of all airport employees soon. We'll check it out and make sure we didn't miss any potential witnesses."

I thanked him and returned to Sophie. We conjectured that perhaps the two women had simply finished their shift and left the airport before the police had arrived. Sophie added a note to her to-do list. She would contact the police later to clarify this matter as well.

So now was there any remaining part of the concourse that we had overlooked? The stairway to the top of the tower was sealed off with highly visible bright orange-colored tape emblazoned with bold, black lettering. The words on the tape sent chills up my spine: CRIME SCENE—DO NOT CROSS.

The stairway and the top of the tower were out of bounds for us, at least for now, but there were still the two unmarked doors near the staircase to investigate. We tried not to appear too suspicious as we casually sauntered over and opened the first door and quickly stepped inside.

It was another bathroom but much nicer than the others at the airport we had seen. We guessed it was for the exclusive use of special passengers or senior airport staff, or something like that. As Sophie followed her standard operating procedure and included in her notebook an inventory of what she found there that might be of later interest to us, I noticed there was an inside door which, when I opened it, led to an adjoining private waiting room. It resembled the private V.I.P. lounges in which I had enjoyed relaxing at a number of airports when I had been on my lecture circuit. Although somewhat smaller than the others, it was still attractively furnished with comfortable sofas and armchairs, a flat screen television and a wet bar. I discovered, merely for investigatory purposes only of course, that the cupboards above the bar were all tightly locked. The floor of the lounge was covered with a soft pile, cream-colored carpeting that nicely complemented the overall color scheme. My goodness, the thoughts in my head were sounding a lot like the restaurant review I had read a little earlier. I realized that I did need some rest. Waiting for Sophie to join me in the lounge, I walked over to an overstuffed armchair and sat down. Looking more closely at the rug from my new angle, I noticed that there were mud stains on the carpet. Probably from someone's shoes. I drew this fact to Sophie's attention when she entered the room a minute or so later.

"You would think they would clean the rug in here, wouldn't you? It would not be very inviting to their special passengers."

"No it wouldn't, Harry. Nor would the tracks you just made across the room to that chair."

I looked where Sophie was pointing. Indeed, without noticing it, my shoes had apparently dirtied the carpet as well. Furthermore, I was shocked to observe that the residue that had just come off the soles of my shoes looked exactly like those pre-existing muddy imprints. What was this all about?

Chapter 12

"Since this is the first time I have ever been in this lounge, I can only assume that someone else with mud and sand on his shoes was walking around in here before me."

While I was busily stating the obvious, Sophie was already on her hands and knees on the carpet. She had removed from the seemingly inexhaustible supply of useful objects she carried in her tote two small plastic bags and a plastic spatula. The bags were not unlike the one in which Robby Donohue had deposited Sally's sparkly cell phone. Sophie scraped a bit of the residue from my shoes into one bag and a similar amount of the gritty material that had previously stained the carpet into the other. She labeled each bag with her pen and then sat down next to me in another armchair.

"Although I'm neither a chemist nor a geologist," I said while wiping the rest of the muddy substance from my shoes with the aid of the paper napkins also from Sophie's treasure trove, "I'll bet you dollars to doughnuts that the muck in these two bags came from the same place."

"They certainly look the same to me," she agreed.

"And that place must be the beach area where I saw Edward digging. And if it had indeed been Edward's shoes that also stained the carpet, why do you think he was in this V.I.P. lounge at all? What was he doing in here?"

"And *when* would he have had the time to come in here at all? Let me check again what Mrs. Gillespie told us," Sophie said as she opened her notebook.

I was not sure I understood exactly what Sophie's question meant but said nothing as she carefully re-read several pages and made a number of additional notations all the while muttering incomprehensible monosyllabic expostulations under her breath. Finally, she turned to me and said quietly, "Harry, it might be that I'm so bushed that I can't think straight, but it looks to me that the timeline just doesn't add up."

"What do you mean, Sophie?"

"Either I've gotten the facts all screwed up or someone we've talked to hasn't told us the truth." She handed me her notebook opened to the page she had just completed.

This is what I read:

AIRPORT TIMELINE

11:00 pm	Edward called Mr. Benson to arrange drive to airport.
12:30 am (?)	Edward arrived at Benson home obviously drunk.
12:45 am	Mr. Benson and Edward left Benson home for 1-hour drive to airport.
1:00 am	We talked to Mrs. Benson at her home then left immediately for airport.
1:45 am	Mr. Benson dropped Edward off at the airport ?

2:00 am	We arrived at the airport.
2:05 am	Mrs. Gillespie told us Edward had just left restaurant via back door.
2:06 am	Cleaning woman told us Edward had just climbed staircase to tower.
2:08 am	Harry called Sophie on cell phone reporting Edward had just jumped.

"So, when did Edward have time to go into the V.I.P. lounge and dirty up the carpet?" Sophie rhetorically asked. "It took us a full hour to drive to the airport from the Benson house and for most of that time Madge was driving like a bat out of hell. I doubt that Noah Benson could have gotten there in less than an hour. Mrs. Benson told us that they left at 12:45. Mrs. Gillespie was also very certain that she opened the locked door to the restaurant at 1:45 and was immediately accosted by Edward. She told us he had only just left by the back door when we entered. A minute or so later he was seen climbing the stairs to the Observation tower. So, I repeat, when did he have time to go into that lounge?"

"Let alone why would he have gone there to begin with?" I added.

"Right. So what are we to make of this?" I could see from Sophie's expression that her brain had begun ticking away at Mach speed as she mused aloud. "Maybe someone other than Edward with the same junk on his shoes as you had on yours went into this lounge and messed up the rug. Could that be possible?" she asked.

"I suppose anything is possible, but the shoe prints on the rug are a bit damp exactly like mine. It would appear whoever was on the beach this night was there about the same time I was. And I sure as hell didn't see anyone there other than Edward. However, it was pitch black out there, and I did give myself a nasty bump on the head when I passed out. So who knows? Of course," I added with a slight smirk and a twinkle in my eye, "if it had been Edward's evil twin who had a penchant for soiling rugs in airport V.I.P. lounges, that would explain everything."

"Oh, easily. Case closed." I was sorry to observe that Sophie's attempt at a smile and a witticism was only half-hearted at best. It was clear the strain of this terrible night was taking its toll on both of us.

"I think we've done about all the sleuthing we are physically and emotionally able to do right now. Let's get back to Havenport and get some shut eye."

"When you're right, you're right, Harry. Give me a minute or two to look more closely around this room and then we can skedaddle out of here." As she quickly prowled around the lounge writing down in her notebook what she found there, I leaned back in the armchair and closed my eyes.

By keeping my eyes tightly shut, I was able to pretend that I didn't see the perspiration that rolled down my father's face or the way his forehead furrowed with concern. By forcing myself to sing softly inside my head my favorite Mickey Mouse Club song, I was able to pretend that I didn't hear my father's labored breathing as he struggled to keep us on course or the scary splintering sound that came from the bottom of the little rowboat . . .

> We are the merry Mouseketeers (Mouseketeers)
> We've got a lot above our ears ('Bove our ears)

My singing inside my head grew louder in order to drown out the fear I pretended not to hear in my father's voice as he tried to convince me that losing the oar was nothing more than a slight inconvenience.

The talents given to you and me
We must develop faithfully
So we can be good Mouseketeers (Mouseketeers)

I mentally sang more and more loudly so that I wouldn't hear him tell me that he was going to swim for help. That I was to remain in the boat.

As we continue through the years (Through the years)
We won't forget the Mouseketeers (Mouseketeers)

"Harrison. Harrison. Listen to me. Stop crying. Be a man. Don't be a baby. Be a man."

Hup, two, three, four
Hooray! Hooray! Hooray!

"Your name is Harrison Hunt. It is the name of a man. Not a baby."

Cheers for the merry Mouseketeers (Mouseketeers)

"Your name is . . .

"Mr. Hunt, Mr. Hunt." The voice calling me prompted me to open my eyes. It was the unfortunately named Officer Krupke. "What are you two doing in here, Mr. Hunt? And how did you get in? This part of the airport is always locked up tight at night."

"Well, it was open when we came in a few minutes ago, officer." Sophie's voice betrayed the irritation she was feeling. "After what we've gone through tonight, we needed a quiet place to unwind and think. I'm sure you can understand."

He certainly did not appear as if he understood, but he said, "Well, all right. But would you mind leaving now, so I can be sure the lounge is securely locked? Thanks very much."

After he closed the door behind him, I turned to Sophie with an air of complete exasperation. "Oh, good. Another mystery we can't explain. 'The Case of the Unlocked Locked Door.' Didn't the Hardy Boys or Nancy Drew solve that one? Let's give them a call in the morning."

"Yes, Harry, let's. They'll certainly be of as much help to us as 'Dear kindly Sergeant Krupke.'" This time Sophie's grin was a bit more heartfelt, and as we left the terminal and walked to Madge's car in the parking lot we both began singing a rousing *West Side Story* tribute to the stalwart officer. We had completed the first verse as we exited the parking lot, the one that includes the immortal lines:

> Dear kindly Sergeant Krupke
> You gotta understand,
> It's just our bringin' up-ke
> That gets us out of hand.

We regaled ourselves with the next several verses while Sophie maneuvered the twisting, mostly unlit roads leading us back to Havenport and the comfortable bedding of the Magill home. Just as I shouted out "I'm depraved on accounta I'm deprived!" Sophie said, "Harry, this road doesn't look a bit familiar to me. I think I may have taken one or two wrong turns." She then gave me a significant look and after a slight but pregnant pause softly said, "I think it would be a good idea. Don't you?"

I knew instantly to what she was referring, and I felt a sudden constriction in my chest added to the dull pain in the back of my head. Not only had I not driven since that awful day in Brookfield, but I had also developed a somewhat uneasy feeling concerning automobile-installed GPS devices. I wouldn't call it a phobia as such although I'm sure Sophie would. It was rather a strong antipathy to the sound of the automated tour director's voice and a stronger reluctance to be controlled by that omniscient mechanical wonder. As the readers of my book learned, Sophie and I had totally relied on one such device which we had anthropomorphically named 'Mandy' during those five eventful days in Brookfield. The result of that slavish reliance almost cost me my life. Since then, whenever I happened to be driven in a vehicle which employed a GPS, I always requested the driver to turn it off, claiming a headache or some such ruse.

I knew that Madge was a devotee of all sorts of mechanical gadgets and therefore had a state of the art model prominently mounted on her car's dashboard. Luckily, she had never encountered the need to employ its assistance when I had ridden with her. It now occurred to me that Sophie might have surreptitiously told Madge of this slight peculiarity of mine, and that was why she had never used it when I was in the car. In any case, the look in Sophie's eye and the kindly, sympathetic smile on her lips were all I needed to know. She wanted to turn on that blasted robot, and I would be forced to hear that voice again and be reminded once more how helpless I had felt during that final, terrifying car chase.

"What do you say, boss? Just this once? We both need to get back to Havenport as soon as possible. I don't want to traipse blindly up and down these mountain roads any more than I have to this morning. And you don't either, do you? Just this once?"

What could I say that would not diminish myself any further in her estimation? Of course my year-long aversion to Mandy and her ilk was ridiculous, irrational. Of course it was. But still a chill went up my spine as I reluctantly said, "All right. If you have to use the damned thing, then go ahead."

And with a grateful smile, she turned it on and typed in Madge's home address. I braced myself for the slightly condescending Mid-Atlantic tones I so well recalled, but when the thing spoke, telling us to take the second right, it was not a female's voice we heard but the clipped, reassuring tones of a British baritone speaking perfect and deferential BBC English. The name 'Manderville' instantly sprang to mind. This was the name of the family butler of Sir Barry James, one of the people who would soon be producing my plays on the West End, and the butler's voice was very similar to the one which now calmly provided the directions we needed. Despite myself, I sighed with relief.

"I really had gotten pretty darned lost, Harry. This is making it so much easier for me. Thanks, boss."

"Of course, my dear Sophie, anything to oblige," I replied magnanimously. I don't think she rolled her eyes in that way of hers when I said that. Although she had every reason to do so, I'm pretty confident she didn't. Have I mentioned how fortunate I am that Sophie is in my life?

Following Manderville's sensible instructions, we soon left the winding back lanes and turned onto the state road. Although it would be a longer way home as the crow flies, (I never did completely understand the meaning of that phrase.) it was certainly a safer one.

The sky very slowly began to lighten as did our spirits. The few buildings we noticed were all tightly shuttered. The one or two gas stations and the miniscule mall we passed were all closed. The only things we could make out in any detail in the mall were what appeared to be a nondescript medical center at one end and an equally, architecturally blah cineplex at the other.

"That must be where Edward and Sally went to the movies tonight, or rather last night, on their ill-fated date," I remarked. "I don't think it will do us any harm to visit that not so palatial Picture Palace later in the day. Maybe we'll learn a thing or two. What do you think, Sophie?"

"Good idea, boss. Remind me to add that to our to-do list when we get home."

My thoughts then turned from the formulaic, rather ugly and strictly utilitarian architecture of the movie theatre at the mall to the true great Movie Palaces I had enjoyed visiting during my lifetime: the Castro in San Francisco that resembled nothing less than a Mexican cathedral, the Native American-art deco masterpiece that was the Kimo in Albuquerque, the neon minarets of Portland's Bagdad (sic) Theater, the gilded emperor poised above the proscenium arch of Grauman's Chinese inscrutably musing on the giants who had indeed once walked the streets of Hollywood leaving their footprints behind in the cement forecourt (as opposed to dirty footprints on an airport's carpeting) and, of course, the Big Apple's Radio City Music Hall where this year's Tony awards would be held. I had begun composing my acceptance speech when Sophie called out, "Look, Harry, that must be the main branch of Mrs. Gillespie's restaurant."

Sure enough, to our left was a substantially larger version of the Cape Cod themed cottage we had visited at the airport. Although its sign was not illuminated now, we could still make out the words Cousin Carrie's Home Style Cooking. Painted sea gulls darted between the letters and a painted lighthouse stood majestically at one end.

"We'll be making another royal visit to her highness there I'm sure," Sophie said. "Maybe we'll be able to get more out of her this time." It was clear that Sophie had no great affection for the formidable Jessie Gillespie.

As we were passing the restaurant, I noticed that it abutted another rather large building. The Copper Moon was apparently some sort of a night club. It was still too dark for us to discern any of the features of the large moon sculpture perched above its front entrance, but our headlights did illuminate a sign that read "Hot Jazz, Cold Drinks."

I wondered if we would ever have the time or the inclination to partake of either while we remained in Havenport. Remembering again the heavy responsibility that Madge Magill had thrust upon my exhausted shoulders brought me back to another reality, and we both became engrossed in our own thoughts until, finally, the *veddy tweedy* tones of Manderville announced that we had reached our destination.

We parked in Madge's driveway just as the sun began to rise over the cliffs in the east. The same cliffs from which a smiling killer had raised his rifle and changed all our lives for ever. With a huge, unmuffled yawn, I wearily managed to open the passenger door and almost jumped out of my skin. Standing immediately in front of me was a tall young man.

"Welcome back, Mr. Hunt. I've been waiting for you."

I first groggily thought it was Edward back from the near dead. But no, it was in fact Patrolman Robby Donohue. And Patrolman Robby Donohue did not seem in a good mood. Not in the least.

AS ROBBY CONTINUED TO PRESS Sophie and me for more and more details about Edward's leap from the tower and our connection with it, my mind, like King Henry IV's, questioned what had I done to deserve such sleepless torture.

> O sleep, O gentle sleep,
> Nature's soft nurse, how have I frighted thee,
> That thou no more wilt weigh my eyelids down
> And steep my senses in forgetfulness?

And then my foggy brain's need to cast blame caused me mentally to curse the young patrolman. Couldn't he see how tired Sophie and I were? My inner Shakespearean voice declaimed that

> Robby does murder sleep, the innocent sleep.
> Sleep that knits up the ravelled sleeve of care,
> The death of each day's life, sore labor's bath,

Balm of hurt minds, great nature's second course,
Chief nourisher in life's feast

Boy, did I need all the bath and balm that I could find. I needed to get rid of Robby before I let slip something that might endanger Edward and Madge. So, I did what I had to do. I giggled like a madman and said quite loudly and with a flourish, "I want to beg, borrow or steal some bed, bath and beyond." This stopped Robby's determined questioning in its tracks and caused both Sophie and him to look at me with some concern.

"Robby, you see how exhausted the boss and I are," she softly said to him pulling him to one side of the driveway. "We both will be in a much better state to answer all your questions, and we realize they are very legitimate questions, after we've gotten some much needed sleep."

To clinch the matter, I then loudly spewed forth a favorite passage from Henry IV, part I:

She bids you on the wanton rushes lay you down
And rest your gentle head upon her lap,
And she will sing the song that pleaseth you
And on your eyelids crown the god of sleep.
Charming your blood with pleasing heaviness,
Making such difference betwixt day and night
The hour before the heavenly-harness'd team
Begins his golden progress in the east.

Even Sophie appeared a bit shocked by my oratorical outburst. But when I gave her a sly wink, a slight smile formed at the corner of her lips. She then turned back to Robby and said in her most distressed manner, "He really needs to go to bed, or I can't promise what will happen to him. Please, Robby, how about it?"

The basically good-natured Robby who actually seemed to have been quite uncomfortable in the role of Mr. District Attorney and certainly had no desire to cart me off to the local sanitorium, slowly nodded and said, "All right, Ms. Xerxes, call me later when you both can think clearly. And we'll start fresh. Please take care of yourself, Mr. Hunt."

"Thank you, Robby, God bless you." Sophie's manner was so serious and seemingly so earnest that I almost busted a gasket trying not to explode with laughter. I managed to get into the house before collapsing on a nearby sofa. Sophie closed the door behind her and clapped her hands together several times. "Very clever, Edwin Booth. Your antic disposition seemed to have worked. But we both better hit the sack before it really is booby hatch time for both of us."

My slight case of hysteria quickly abated and agreeing with her we slowly walked up the stairs to our bedrooms. At the door of mine I said, "We need to decide what and how much we want to tell the police and work out what our course of action is going to be. But first, "To sleep, perchance to dream."

"I hear you, boss. I hear you." were the last words my tired brain absorbed before I greeted my pillow and oblivion.

The knocking on the door brought me back to semi-consciousness. I was surprised that when I awoke these words were in my brain and on my lips: "Last scene of all, that ends this strange eventful history, is second childishness and mere oblivion. Sans teeth, sans eyes, sans taste, sans everything."

When Sophie entered my room, the look on her face brought me sharply back to life. "Sorry to wake you, Harry. It's Annabelle Laurence on the phone. She wants to talk to you."

"Why in blazes is she calling me at the crack of . . ."

"Nine, actually. And she wouldn't tell me. She said it was very important that she talk only with you."

"No rest for the weary!" I moaned. "All right, all right. I'll be right there. She'll just have to hold her horses for a minute."

"Grumble, grumble, grumble, you big phony," Sophie laughed. "The nearest extension is in Edward's room."

As I crossed the room, I stumbled on my jacket which I had haphazardly tossed on the floor when I had gone to bed and painfully twisted my ankle. "Just what I damn well needed," I muttered as I hobbled as quickly as I could manage down the hallway and into Edward Magill's bedroom. I quickly glanced around the room to locate the land phone. The room was as neat and orderly as it always was. As neat and orderly and organized and sane as Edward had always seemed. How could this quiet, kindly, studious young man be a murderer? How could he have tried and very nearly succeeded in taking his own life? As I reached for the phone, I noticed a nearby wall lined with awards: National Honor Society certificates and other scholastic accolades, science fair first prizes, trophies for junior chess and debating tournament championships. As I picked up the phone, I gasped. I spied on a low shelf what looked like . . . I would investigate further after I curtailed this phone call.

"Good morning, Miss Laurence. This is Harrison Hunt."

"Oh, yes, Mr. Hunt. Good morning. Thank you so much for speaking to me. After what I understand you have gone through since I last saw you at our little rehearsal yesterday afternoon, I am sure social chit-chat with an old lady is not high on your list of priorities."

"Not at all, Miss Laurence. What can I do for you?" Annabelle Laurence was a gracious, lovely woman who had of course achieved many social and artistic successes in Havenport. Her charming humility did much to smooth my ruffled feathers this morning. She soon almost made me forget the pain in my ankle as well as the dull throbbing in the back of my head which I now realized had returned.

"I wouldn't be at all surprised, and it would certainly be justified, after all you have been put through last night and early this morning, if you just slammed down this phone in dismay and disgust at my presumption in making this request of you, poor sweet you."

"Request?"

"Yes. I foolishly and now I see very selfishly felt I could ask you to do something, something very important to me, in fact to the whole village. But I see now how inconsiderate it was for me to entertain this thought. I am so sorry to disturb you in this very sad time, Mr. Hunt. Please forgive me."

"Not at all, Miss Laurence. What is it you would like me to do for you?"

"Well, if it wouldn't be too much trouble for a man as busy as you are, Mr. Hunt, it crossed my mind that this Thursday evening, in addition to the small performance of Shakespearean scenes the Little Players will be performing, the scenes for which you have already so kindly and expertly provided us with your invaluable knowledge and insight . . ."

"Are you thinking of something additional for the performance?"

"Yes, I am, Mr. Hunt. Tom Wright was much loved in Havenport. The entire village is in a state of shock over his sudden and tragic death. I think it would be of great assistance to the community not only for the performance to be dedicated to his memory but also a memorial tribute be presented by the Players in his honor. A series of additional speeches or short scenes to celebrate Tom's life and express our love and fellowship for him. And who better than the Bard of Avon himself to compose these tributes, and who better than the great

Shakespearean scholar and director Mr. Harrison Hunt to plan, put together and direct this memorial? Do I presume too much, Mr. Hunt? Am I too selfishly reprehensible in requesting the use of your valuable time and talent in this noble cause? Am I, my dear Mr. Hunt?"

By the time I hung up the phone, I not only had agreed to be responsible for the whole shebang but also to hold the first of the daily rehearsals this evening at Laurence House.

Sophie joined me in Edward's room so quickly after Miss Laurence's closing remark: "I can no other answer make, but, thanks, and thanks, and thanks" that it was obvious that she had been listening to the entire conversation on the other phone.

"Let me guess," she smirked, *As You Like It?*

"Actually, my dear Sophie, the gracious and erudite Miss Laurence's parting expression of gratitude is from *Twelfth Night*.

"Well, excuuuuse me," she laughed in her best Steve Martin impersonation. "Whatever it was from, it was a fitting ending to a masterful performance. You must be covered with whitewash."

"Whitewash?"

"Sure, Tom Sawyer Laurence certainly got you to paint that fence of hers."

"Really, Sophie. I thought you admired Miss Laurence as much as I."

"I do, Harry. But let's face it. That lady can wrap you around her little finger."

"Oh, well, it will be a nice gesture to hold a loving memorial to Tom," I said. "And I hope it will provide a needed respite for us from that other request made for me last night by Madge. It's not easy being God's deputy, that's for sure."

"I'm with you on that score," Sophie sighed and then said, "Well, I think we should start working out our plans of attack. I brought my trusty little notebook. Let's go over in detail all we know about Tom's murder, about Sally's disappearance and Edward's possible involvement with both. We'll also need to devise our strategy for when we face Robby again later today. Also, let's go over our to-do list and . . . What are you doing over there, Harry?"

"I think we should begin by going over Edward's room with a fine tooth comb, Sophie. Who knows what possible clues we'll find, and we can most assuredly begin right here." I pointed to the small shelf I had spotted as I began to speak with Miss Laurence. "Look at these half dozen trophies, Sophie. They're all awards that Edward won for outstanding achievement in marksmanship."

Sophie bent down to look more closely at the trophies. "They're shaped like miniature . . ." She froze in astonishment and then slowly stood up and turned to me. I could barely hear her say, "My God, Harry. Edward's an expert shot with a rifle."

Chapter 14

THE LOOK OF HORROR ON Sophie's face mirrored my own as she studied Edward's rifle-shaped trophies. "They re all from a number of rifle club tournaments in Washington State," she said.

"Of course, Sophie. Madge told us that Edward's father took him hunting when he visited him. He must have acquired his skill up there."

"I wonder what kind of hunting he's been doing. The guy who fired at us in the boat must have been an expert shot. Oh, Harry, what if Edward really did kill Tom and . . . and Sally too?"

"Sophie, it's too early to make any decisions on the matter. Besides, we don't know for sure that Sally is actually dead."

"Then what was in that canvas wrapping you saw Edward bury?"

"That is just what we are going to find out once and for all. And the sooner the better. I suggest we go back to the shoreline and try to locate that spot again now that the sun is up. It may be like trying to find that proverbial haystack needle, but I think we should try." I looked at Sophie for approval of this seemingly hopeless plan. I got it.

"I'm with you all the way, Harry. But let's grab something to eat first. I can barely remember what food tastes like."

I seconded the motion, but first a quick detour into the bathroom for a hot shower. Ye gods, how I needed that. But what I definitely did not need was to see the worn and ragged visage that looked back at me in the bathroom mirror as I shaved. As if I needed any further proof of the ravaging effects that last night's events had had on me. I looked like hell or rather like Shakespeare's seventh and final age of man. I might as well have been "sans teeth, sans eyes, sans taste, sans everything." It was strange that this quote was once again in my mind. Oh well, the vanity mirror's brutal attack on my vanity plus the nagging ankle pain from this morning's misadventure in the bedroom and the persistence of the throbbing in the back of my head from last night's ridiculous fall all quickly removed the restorative effects of the hot water. With a deepening sense of doom, I hobbled down the stairs to meet Sophie in the kitchen before embarking on our fool's errand to the beach.

The tempting aroma of bacon frying started my taste buds salivating despite my gloomy mood. Good old Sophie, I thought as I entered the kitchen. But noticing who was working up a storm at the stove, I said with surprise, "Well, good morning, Mrs. Donohue."

"Good morning to you, Mr. Hunt. Now you sit right down at the table next to Miss Sophie there, and I'll fix you a breakfast you'll never forget. You are hungry, I hope?"

"Am I!" I exclaimed. As we both wolfed down the scrumptious waffles smothered in maple syrup, slabs of crispy bacon, sweet potato biscuits served with homemade cranberry preserves, orange juice (freshly squeezed) and hot strong coffee (freshly brewed), Mrs. Donohue related to us the details of the phone call she had received from Madge this morning. From the hospital Madge had told her what had happened at the airport and that Edward remained in very serious condition in intensive care. She had also asked her to take care of Mr. Hunt and Miss Sophie and see to all their needs because (and she looked strangely at me as she quoted Madge) "our Heavenly Father has sent Mr. Hunt to discover the truth."

Trying to sidestep this awkward moment I said, "Well I can not guarantee that I have been sent from heaven, but this delicious breakfast certainly has. Thank you so much, Mrs. Donohue."

"My pleasure, Mr. Hunt. Mrs. Magill has always been so kind to me I'll gladly do anything she asks. And Edward is like another son to me. He and Robby have always been like brothers. So whatever I can do to help you help him . . . well, you just have to ask."

"Thank you, Mrs. Donohue." I was touched by her sincerity.

Sophie then asked, "You've been with the Magill family for a long time?"

"Yes, I have. Indeed I have." As she poured more coffee for Sophie and a second helping of everything for me, she told us that her mother and father had been employed by Madge's parents as housekeeper and gardener. They lived in the little cottage behind the main house. Little Edna had been born in that cottage and grew up there assisting her parents in their duties. "The property was much larger then, you understand," she said while slicing the cinnamon buns she had just taken out of the oven. The estate had originally contained over thirty beautiful acres of meadows and woodlands. But as times grew harder and the mill and cannery closed down, the family had no choice but to sell more and more sections of their land. Madge and Edna played together as girls, grew up and eventually each married.

"I was luckier with my Hank than Mrs. Magill was with that fella from New York City," she added sadly. Both families had sons born two months apart. After Mrs. Donohue's parents had died, she and Hank had taken over their responsibilities. Little Robby had grown up in the cottage as his mother had. He became good friends with young Edward. The two boys were inseparable when the Magills came from the City to visit.

"But there was no hiding the fact that there was trouble brewing between Mrs. Magill and that husband of hers. He resented that she had taken that job at Yale University. He wouldn't move out of New York, and she was forced to take the train back and forth every day. There were other problems as well." Mrs. Donohue's face was impassive as she made this last comment.

She quickly continued with her story. The Magills had divorced. He moved to the state of Washington; she moved to New Haven. Madge and Edward spent every summer in Havenport as Edward and Robby grew to young manhood. Ten years ago, Madge's folks had died in a plane crash only a month after Hank Donohue had his fatal heart attack. "That was a terrible time for all of us. Just terrible." She brushed away any stray tear from her eyes in a matter-of-fact manner and continued her history as she washed the breakfast dishes. She had thanked Sophie for offering to help but said it was "No trouble, honey. No trouble at all."

Madge had inherited the property from her parents. She remained in Connecticut during the school year, but she and Edward returned to Havenport each summer. To help pay for the upkeep of the estate that encompassed only three and a half acres now, Madge engaged a realtor to rent the property from September to May. Mrs. Donohue stayed on as housekeeper "and to keep an eye on the tenants," she added. The renters had liked the home so much they had offered to buy it from Madge, but she had refused. Her dream was to move there permanently when she retired. Her dream had been fulfilled last month. "We all thought everything would be so perfect." There was no stopping the tears now as she concluded, "And then this terrible thing with the Wrights and poor Edward . . ."

"Try not to worry, Mrs. Donohue," Sophie said consolingly. "Mr. Hunt and I will do everything we can to get this mess straightened out. Try not to worry."

"I know you will. Thank you. Thank you both. Well, I've got work to do before church, and I bet you do as well." With one determined brush at her face with her apron the tears were removed, and Mrs. Donohue was all business again. She left us in the kitchen on her way to the vacuum cleaner.

"That was quite the family saga. Something like a cross between *Gone with the Wind* and *Wuthering Heights*," I said with a laugh. "What did she mean about 'other troubles' between Madge and her husband?"

"There had been rumors at the time that Ethan Magill was involved in some shady financial doings before he upped and left everything for the wild west, but I don't think it ever went beyond the rumor stage. I had always suspected that he was a bit of a womanizer as well, but who knows?"

Before Sophie had the chance to offer more hypotheses, I heard the distinctive tones of the Fifth Brandenburg Concerto. I reached behind my chair on which I had draped my jacket and retrieved my cell phone from the jacket pocket. I was surprised that when I flipped the phone open there was no one on the line. The familiar ringtone then once again sounded.

"Boss, that's not your phone," Sophie said pointing to the one in my hand. Indeed I could detect now that the sound of the ringing came from upstairs.

"Then whose phone do I have?" I sat there bewildered as Sophie marched up the stairs to my bedroom. I looked more closely at the phone I was holding. I saw now that although similar looking, it was actually a different make and model from mine. So what was it doing in my pocket?

Sophie rejoined me in the kitchen a few minutes later. "Here's your phone, Harry. It was on your bedside table. I missed answering the call. But, as you see, that might be all for the best."

I clicked on the "Missed Call" message on the face of my phone and saw that the recent call had been from Barbara Wright. I agreed with Sophie that I did not want to talk to Barbara right now. What could I tell her about her missing daughter? We needed some facts. And we needed them now.

"She'll probably be calling me next," Sophie prophesied. Right on cue her cell phone rang. Taking it out, she looked at the caller's identification and nodded grimly at me.

"Well, Nostradamus," I said, "I suggest you hold off answering it until we have something concrete to tell Barbara."

"When you're right, you're right, Harry. Let's go find what's buried on the beach. Maybe it will be a treasure chest of gold doubloons," she laughed. "They say that pirates used to frequent the harbor."

"Let us hope it's anything except . . ." I left the statement incomplete. Sophie knew what I had been thinking. "Shall we walk there or take the car?" she asked.

I suggested that we use the car to haul any implements we could find for digging. As we followed the sounds of the vacuum cleaner, Sophie asked me about the new phone that had mysteriously appeared. I told her I had no idea how it had gotten in my jacket pocket. I could only surmise that in all the chaos we had experienced last night I must have mistakenly picked up someone else's phone.

"What do you say we deal with this new mystery at a later date?" I begged. "How much new information can I take in at any one time? I think it was Francis Bacon who wisely said: 'The desire for knowledge in excess caused man to fall." Gingerly touching the back of my head I added ruefully, "Heaven knows I have fallen more than enough lately, thank you very much." With a chuckle, Sophie agreed.

We interrupted Mrs. Donohue's housecleaning to ask her if we could borrow a shovel. We went with her to the basement and selected two sturdy ones. Mrs. Donohue once more looked strangely at us but asked no questions. We put the shovels in the trunk and were ready to start off when my phone rang again.

When I removed it from my jacket pocket, I realized I once more had selected the wrong cell phone. With a snarl, I reached into my other pocket and pulled out *my* cell phone. Before answering it, I noticed who was calling me. "Oh no, Sophie," I cried, "look who it is. We can't keep ignoring the poor woman."

"Let me take it, boss," said the saintly Sophie. Saint Sophia, patron saint of lost causes and cowardly employers. "Bless you," I said handing her the phone.

"Hello, Barbara, how's it going?" Sophie looked at me with a face full of self-recrimination as she searched for some excuse to hold Barbara off for now. But it sounded as if she didn't have to manufacture any more evasions. "What, Barbara? Really, Barbara? You are, Barbara? We'll try, Barbara. We'll do our best, Barbara. Yes, we will, Barbara. All right, Barbara. Good bye, Barbara."

"Was that Barbara?" I deadpanned.

"You'll never guess, Harry. She's on her way back to Havenport and wants us to join her at the old church at noon."

"Now I have to go to church and lie in front of God and all His angels and all His hosts!"

"I told Barbara we'll do our best to meet her there. Maybe we won't have to lie. Maybe we'll have found some truths by the time we see her."

"Maybe so," I said. But I didn't believe it for a minute.

"You better give me that other cell phone to hold on to. We don't need any further confusion." I fully concurred. We certainly have had enough of that commodity to last a lifetime. Sophie put the phone in her tote bag after noting that the mystery cell phone's battery required charging. We walked to Madge's car and drove the short distance till we reached the general store.

"All right. Now let me think. I started from here in the direction I believed Edward had taken," I said. "Toward the water." Sophie drove one more block. The seashore was now right in front of us. It was time to retrace my steps as well as I could. What would we find? I took a deep breath and got out of the car.

Chapter 15

I REMOVED THE TWO SHOVELS from the trunk and waited for Sophie to join me. It took her a moment or two longer than it should have. I assumed that the seriousness of what we might find buried this morning had given her a momentary pause. But she seemed resolute as she took one of the cases from me, and we set off.

I was glad that we had chosen the tri-fold camping shovels we had seen in the basement. Although sturdily constructed of heavy duty steel, they cleverly folded into their olive drab canvas covers that we now wore like back packs. They should not attract any undue attention from passersby. Not that we saw many people. The fishing boats did not usually set out on Sundays, and the early morning hour and overcast sky seemed to relinquish the rocky beach pretty much to ourselves and to our solitary and increasingly sobering thoughts.

We descended the long flight of ancient wooden steps I had walked down last night to get on the beach and then turned in the general direction I had taken. But whether or not we were following Edward's path exactly was unclear. It had been so dark, and I had

had only the penlight's narrow beam for illumination. I remembered that after walking pretty much in this direction for some time I had heard faint panting and digging sounds somewhere to my right. I had followed those sounds till I had suddenly seen Edward in the distance. It was then that I had collapsed for some reason, dropped and lost the penlight. After I came back to consciousness, I had walked the twenty or thirty feet to the spot where Edward had been but could find nothing. Then, I had turned left and slightly aided by the backlight of my uncooperative cell phone somehow managed to get back to the road.

Not that I wanted to blame Sophie for all of this, but if the flashlight she had handed me hadn't been the smallest one mankind had ever produced, we might not be in this fix. If I could only catch sight of it, I believed I could retrace my steps to the burial spot. *To see* or *not to see* that damned penlight, *that* was the question, thank you very much, your royal gloomy Danish highness!

To belabor this thought a bit more, my wandering mind then streamed to the theme song of the smashing Canadian television series *Slings & Arrows* that Sophie and I had so enjoyed. The opening lyrics to the theme caught the irreverent attitude of the show's Shakespearean actors. I sang with as full a voice as I could:

Cheer up Hamlet
Chin up Hamlet
Buck up you melancholy Dane
So your uncle is a cad
Who murdered Dad and married Mum
That's really no excuse to be as glum as you've become . . .

"Not that I want to interrupt," Sophie nevertheless interrupted, "but instead of howling our brains out, we might want to take a more productive approach." Before I had the chance to become deeply offended by her words, she went on, "It seems to me we've been going at this the wrong way around. From what you've told me, Harry, it was hearing Edward make those sounds that enabled you to find him. And when you did and sadly lost him again, you turned away from the ocean and walked towards the road until you managed to climb up onto it."

"Yes, that's right. Then I turned left again heading back toward the general store."

"So, wouldn't it be better if we start off where Madge and I picked you up and then return from there back to the beach. We should then be closer I would think to the spot we want to find."

I agreed with her faultless logic, and we turned our backs to the water and started trudging through the sand and dirt once again. When we both stopped for a moment to take off our shoes and dump the detritus from them, I noted that the consistency of the residue adhering to the soles of mine was now markedly different from before. It made it clearer to me that whoever had visited the airport lounge this morning had also been here last night with me. If Sophie's timetable were correct, it seemed that this person couldn't have been Edward. As we started walking again, I scratched the back of my head in bewilderment. I couldn't explain how this conundrum had occurred; I only knew that it had.

I instantly regretted fingering that sore portion of my skull. Noticing my not so quiet yelp of pain, Sophie gave me one of her severe looks. "I'm really concerned about that bump on your noggin, Harry. I meant to ask Mrs. Donohue this morning for the name of a doctor she recommended. In fact, before you talk me out of it again, I'm going to give her a call right now."

Although I would not give Sophie the satisfaction of agreeing with her, I was beginning to be concerned about this head injury as well. So I merely exhaled a dramatic sigh of bemused exasperation as Sophie reached in her tote bag for a cell phone. She had quite a selection from which to choose.

"You know, I'm lugging around *three* frigging phones," she complained, "mine, yours, and the surprise mystery guest. Here take yours back and this time try not to use the camera so much. It's no wonder your battery is always in such precarious shape."

"What do you mean?" I immediately replied in a huff. "I don't think I've ever used that ridiculous camera mysteriously built into my phone. If they spent all their time and energy perfecting the core telephonic component instead of adding one unnecessary feature after another, like a camera and heaven knows what else, I would have been able to reach help immediately last night instead of wandering around the desert like the Israelites for forty . . ."

"Your head must be even worse than I feared, Harry, if you don't remember taking all these photographs."

"What in the name of blazes are you jabbering about, Sophie?" I bellowed.

"Look right here, Mr. Self-Control. This number indicates how many shots were taken. See, twenty-two."

Grabbing my phone brusquely from her, I was a bit chagrinned to see that Sophie was not as delusional as I had originally conjectured. My cell phone had apparently indeed snapped that many photos. But when were they taken, and who had taken them? I certainly had not done so. I told Sophie as much.

"Well, let's take a look at them and see what we discover." She pressed one or two little buttons. Immediately the phone's LCD screen sprang into life and revealed the first picture. But what in the name of Beelzebub was it?

"Can you make out what that is, Sophie?" I asked while squinting my eyes.

"Well, it certainly is dark and blurry."

"The understatement of the month! Not only do these blasted Silicon Valley geniuses fail to produce a mobile telephone that consistently works, but they have the effrontery to add insult to injury by including a so-called camera that pales in comparison to my grandfather's original and prototypical Brownie . . ."

I was getting on quite an enjoyable roll when Sophie inconsiderately and inconceivably started chuckling.

"Something funny, my dear Sophie?" I glowered,

"Sorry, boss. But after looking at the whole series of pictures, I think I know what they are and how they got there."

"Well, my hat will be off to you if you do," I responded skeptically. "They look like a collection of dark blobs."

"You told me that after you lost the flashlight you were able to maneuver in the dark by cleverly flipping open the front of the phone and using the screen's backlight to guide your way."

"That's right. It was a dim little guide to be sure, and the blasted light automatically extinguished itself after twenty seconds."

"So you frequently had to flip open the cover to access the light."

"Yes, it was a damned nuisance I can tell you."

"I'm sure it was, Harry. Now don't blow your stack when I tell you this." She began her infernal chuckling again. "I think each time you flipped open the phone . . ." The chuckles were turning into guffaws. ". . . you accidentally and unconsciously took a picture. The little button that activates the camera's shutter is next to the hinge for the cover." The guffaws evolved into weird cackles. "If there had been any other people nearby, they would have been astounded to see you walking in the dark taking little flash pictures every few yards or so." The cackles were now punctuated by extremely unflattering little snorts.

In stony silence I waited until the cackles slowly devolved down to mild snickers and then finally stopped altogether. Wiping her eyes with a tissue, Sophie deservedly appeared rather shamefaced as she apologized: "Sorry about that, boss. I guess I needed a good laugh right about then."

"Well," I magnanimously responded, "I hope it was therapeutic. If rather ridiculous. However, now that we know that I took photos of my route back to the road, perhaps we can use them to our advantage."

We sat down on a large, uncomfortable granite outcropping and slowly and carefully studied the pictures. Most of them were very dark and difficult to decipher. Only one was brightly lit. It looked exactly like a huge white smokestack standing above two enormous black tires. When I described this to Sophie, the cackling began all over again. Once more it took enormous patience on my part to wait out the idiotic laughter. She finally was able to say, "Sorry, Harry. But in this shot you obviously had the lens pointed in the opposite direction. That's a picture of your nose in wide screen and cinemascope." I made no further mention of that unfortunate shot.

After some time, we managed to unravel the meaning of many of the photos. We had to consider them in reverse order I remembered the final time I had used the cell phone for a light source. I had just reached the road and needed to look around to gain my bearings. The resultant photo appeared to be a close-up of something wooden on which some black letters and numbers had been stamped or painted. The picture was dark, but the identification number or whatever it was seemed to begin with HR09. There were other numbers or letters following, but they were illegible. The rest of the photos seemed to be of the patches of ground which happened to be in front of me each time the flash went off. Several rather distinctive stone outcroppings like the one we were now using as a bench seemed identifiable as well as some large bushes, odd shaped dunes and the like. Looking around in all directions, we could detect none of these within immediate sight of where we were now situated.

Rather than continue wandering haphazardly hoping to find one or more of these barely identifiable photographic landmarks, I suggested that we return to the car and then drive the harbor road once again until we located that wooden object with the black lettering depicted in the final photograph. We knew that it must be somewhere on the side of the road between the first set of wooden stairs (a block from the general store) from which I had climbed down to the beach and the next wooden stairway located about a mile or two away. I had reached the road at the end of my travail last night by climbing a steep natural incline. I had never seen any sign of the second stairway

As we walked back the way we had come, we had the first chance in almost twenty-four hours to discuss in any detail what we had experienced since yesterday afternoon. I confessed that I had been ready to follow Robby Donohue's advice and leave Havenport as quickly as possible after the murder in the boat. I didn't want to take the chance that the killer had actually been after Sophie or me. But now this whole situation with Edward and Sally seemed to cloud the issue. Despite what Robby had hypothesized, it now seemed possible that Tom had been the intended victim after all. I now felt sure we had to stay in the village and do all we could to discover the truth. Especially after Madge's request. Would the truth vindicate a mother's faith in her son? It didn't seem likely. Sophie told me her emotional roller coaster ride had begun with the conviction that *she* had been the rifleman's target. But now she too was unsure about that.

The mention of Madge's request to me prompted us to talk a bit about the second request I had received this morning: Miss Annabelle Laurence's request. We tossed around a number of ideas about the memorial program we would put together. We had a lot of work to do before its presentation Thursday evening. Sophie made copious notes.

As we neared the stairs, our thoughts naturally led to poor Sally and what might have happened to her. Sophie told me more of what Barbara Wright had said when she asked us to meet her at the church at noon or actually what she had not said. Strangely, in their brief telephone conversation, Barbara hadn't mentioned whether or not she had called Sally's girlfriends this morning. In fact, she hadn't mentioned Sally at all. She had, however, said that she had a request to make of me.

"Oh no, a third request!" I called out when Sophie mentioned this. "What more superhuman effort must I have to make? And then will there be a fourth request, a fifth? I thought our trip to Havenport was supposed to be a rest for both of us. Some rest!"

Sophie failed to proffer the sympathetic response I had expected. When I turned to look at her, I saw that her back was toward me, and it had noticeably stiffened.

"What's wrong, Sophie?"

"Oh, Harry, I thought all that was finally over."

"What do you mean?"

"I just felt that same old feeling again, that someone was watching me. Oh good, just what I needed, right?"

Looking in all directions and not seeing anyone at all, I replied, "Just what we both needed."

We walked the remaining distance to the car in silence. After returning the canvas cases containing the shovels to the trunk, we rode up the harbor road slowly counting off all the possible objects made of wood that might be the subject of my photo # 22. We had clocked a little over two miles on the odometer when we reached the second set of stairs. Sophie made a U-turn and then parked. I read off the list I had compiled and written down in Sophie's notebook as she had slowly driven. We had passed sixteen large trees, four telephone poles, and five fence posts of various shapes and sizes.

Since I had been walking back in a westward direction when the picture had been snapped, we hoped the lettering we now sought would be visible to us while driving in the same direction. Sophie started the car once again and at a snail's pace we drove back. It was clear when we neared several of the items on my list that they weren't what we were seeking. Others though were possible candidates. So Sophie stopped the car and I hopped out, crossed the street and examined the tree or the fence post in great detail. We found nothing until we reached the first telephone pole. There was black lettering on it about waist high. I ran out in great expectation. Carrying the cell phone with me, I compared its coded number with what I could make out from the picture. The number stenciled on this pole read: HR102A4. The number in the photo began with HR09. Close but no Kewpie doll.

We drove quickly till we reached the second pole. I ran out and read its number: HR101A4. There were two poles left. Showing off my mathematical wizardry to Sophie, I concluded that it was the final pole that I had photographed. We brazenly trusted my intellectual acumen and breezed by the intermediary pole without giving it a second look. Reaching the remaining pole, Sophie parked, and we both got out and were jubilant when we read aloud: HR099A4. Hurrah, Mazel Tov, Q.E.D.

Now what should we do? After retrieving the folding shovels encased in their canvas covers, we began walking down the steep incline that descended below the portion of the road where the telephone pole was positioned. Studying photo # 21, we knew we now were looking for a large oddly-shaped rock adjacent to what appeared to be a small tree or large bush. It took us six or seven minutes, but we found it. As we found many but not all of the topographical features immortalized by my not so award-winning photographs. However, the goddess of good fortune was smiling on us and we managed, somehow, to retrace last night's route. Take that, Hansel and Gretel. Who needs your soggy bread crumbs! Suddenly, eagle-eyed Sophie shouted, "Isn't that your penlight, Harry?"

It was indeed sadly sticking its little head out of the stony soil. And from there I was able to orient myself and led Sophie about thirty feet to the place where I now was certain I had watched Edward digging that hole.

Suddenly the mood changed. Cole Porter put it best: "But how strange the change/ From major to minor." Of course on cue a chill wind began to blow, and the sky began to darken ominously. "Oh please, who needs these melodramatic touches?" I rhetorically queried the heavens as we removed the shovels from their cases. Seeing the discarded canvas on the ground instantly triggered an association in my mind with the canvas package we felt assured was buried somewhere below where we now stood.

With a little shiver of dread, I took my shovel in hand and began to dig. Sophie did likewise a little ways from where I had begun. It was not easy work. The ground was hard, but we persevered. And before we knew it, we had dug a hole a few feet deep. As we both took a short break to stretch our muscles, we stood up and saw that without being aware of it the hole we were digging was about six feet long. Cue the organ music.

Another shudder or two, and we were back at work. Sophie was better at this job than I was, but I did my part. We were both sweating profusely from the exertion despite the cold gusts of wind that had caused the temperature to drop substantially. And then, suddenly, there was a thump as Sophie's shovel hit something. We looked at each other for a long moment and then really put our backs into it.

Finally, we reached the canvas wrappings. I forced myself to step down into the hole and with great trepidation slowly moved the canvas aside. With a gasp, we saw what Edward had buried. It was not Sally.

CHAPTER 16

NO, IT WAS NOT SALLY'S body. It was not a body at all. But in some ways it was just as bad, just as incriminating for Edward. After Sophie and I fully examined what Edward had buried, we stood next to the gaping hole leaning on our shovels deep in thought. So what should we do now? Go to the police? Tell them what we had uncovered, literally? Or should we keep mum about the whole matter, cover up the hole again and finally start minding our own business. Even if that meant withholding evidence, we would still be protecting our dear friend Madge from further heartbreak and anguish. I had pledged to do everything I could to help her and her son. I could see no way that revealing what we had found could do anything but pull the noose even tighter around poor Edward's neck. It seemed unlikely that he would ultimately survive his massive injuries, despite his mother's assurance that it was heaven's will that he would pull through. Did we have the right to destroy his reputation in his mother's eyes as well?

"You know what is really crazy, Sophie? Madge called me God's deputy. Little did we know that in a sense she was right. I am now being required to play God. Do I put Edward's life—what remained of it—in further, greater jeopardy by showing what we've dug up to Robby? Or do I not? Should we instead follow Robby's sensible advice and beat a hasty retreat away from this place and let what happens happen without any further interference from us? To tell or run like hell, that is the question."

"I think you know what the right answer is. Don't you, Harry?"

Another gust of cold wind swept over us both as I looked into Sophie's eyes and slowly, sadly nodded. And then I heard the sound of footsteps, looked up and realized my choice of action had just been taken away from me. Patrolman Robby Donohue was walking towards us. His body language matched the grim expression on his face.

The ironic tone that inflected his first words to us took me by surprise: "Good morning, again, Mr. Hunt, Miss Xerxes. Building sand castles, are you?"

"I wish we were, Robby. Oh, how I wish we were," I said quietly and moved aside as he stepped down into the hole and examined the cache of weapons that Edward had buried there.

As he removed all the objects from the hole and deposited them one by one on the ground, he identified each in his notebook. Sophie had already entered the basic description in her notebook, but Robby's entries appeared to be much more detailed.

Sophie's very rudimentary list read as follows:

3 rifles of different lengths, sizes, manufacturers
2 pistols of different sizes, manufacturers
2 boxes of ammunition
3 sets of targets
3 optical devices (scopes?)
1 pair of protective glasses
2 khaki-colored mats of some sort

1 wooden box containing supplies (for gun cleaning?): aluminum rods, bottles of solvent and oil, patches, etc.

Note: the 5 firearms and wooden box are monogrammed EM!!!

"You know that these all belong to Edward Magill?" Robby asked us while wrapping everything back in the canvas.

"Yes, we do, Robby," Sophie replied. "We noticed the monograms."

"So, why were you burying them?"

Robby's question caught us both off guard. Sophie got her breath back first.

"Burying them? We just got finished UN-burying them!"

"And why were you doing that?"

Before we could respond, he continued. "It's high time we all go down to the station house and talk about all this in great detail. We should have gone there last night I'm afraid. Take the shovels with you." Without saying another word, he hoisted the heavy load on his shoulders. With a succinct head movement indicating we were to follow him, he retraced his steps across the sand.

What could we do? With heavy hearts we followed him. To where I wondered, as had Macbeth, "to the crack of doom?" Probably, eventually. But not just yet. First, we followed Robby to his police car which was parked directly in front of our vehicle on the harbor road. He must have seen it there and then come looking for us. At least he had the kindness not to manacle us. That would have been some photograph to grace the front page of *The New York* Times or, even worse, *Variety*. I could see the headline now:

KOPS KUFF BIG SHOT BOUND FOR BIG HOUSE

And that is just what I had considered myself: a big shot, Mr. Big Shot. I had made the most heinous mistake any person suddenly thrust into the public spotlight could make: I had believed my own press. I had bought hook, line and sinker all the puffery that had been written about me. "A Sherlock Holmes for the 21st century" indeed. Nonsense, Rubbish., Crapola. And I had fallen for it. No, my pride had fallen for it. And I had risked not only my own life because of it but Sophie's as well. Not only once in Brookfield but now, once again, in Havenport. Perhaps if I had called Robby back immediately after I saw Edward sneak away with his canvas-packaged arsenal on his back instead of trying to follow him myself, Edward might not be fighting for his life right this very minute. But no, my pride, my overweening pride had caused me to think that I indeed was God's deputy, that I could solve the mystery where the police, the authorities, the experts could not. The arrogance! As Shakespeare said of Achilles: "He is so plaguy proud that the death-tokens of it/ Cry 'No-recovery.'"

I sat there in the tiny police station crestfallen, humiliated, silently berating myself in this way while Sophie almost single-handedly fielded all of Robby's questions. Here and there I responded when directly addressed, but for the most past Sophie told Robby everything that we had learned—or rather conjectured. My sudden plummeting mood swing made me now second-guess and doubt all the seeming contradictions that Sophie and I had unearthed. (Oh, that terrible word!) Robby dismissed as irrelevant and preposterous all the inconsistencies that Sophie mentioned to him: the troubling timeline, the vanishing cleaning women, the sighting of Noah Benson's limo after Edward's suicide attempt, the carpet stains in the airport lounge.

"Let me level with you two," Robby finally said quietly and rather sadly. "I shouldn't be telling you this, but if you keep this information to yourselves, I think it will help all of us in the long run. The state police are pretty certain they know what's been going on. They're pretty certain that it was Edward who killed Tom Wright and that he's done something as well to Sally. Maybe he killed her as well. After I saw the evidence they found on the cliff this morning and the bullet taken from Tom's body, I'm afraid I have to side with them. Even though Edward is and always has been a good friend of mine, I believe he did these terrible things."

Sophie and I looked at each other for a moment rife with emotion and then turned back to Robby as he continued. "The state police . . . and I . . . believe that when Edward picked Sally up for their date yesterday they quarreled. It seems likely that Sally had followed her parents' wishes and told Edward they should stop seeing each other or that their relationship had become too serious, or something like that. In any case, a struggle seems to have taken place. Evidence was found in Sally's room that seems to support this."

"You mean the smashed cell phone?" Sophie asked.

"That's right, Miss Xerxes. I guess you must have spotted it after I put it in the plastic bag."

Sophie nodded, and Robby went on, "Edward's story that Sally used her cell phone to call one of her girlfriends to get a ride back home from the movies therefore couldn't be true. We've phoned all her friends. No one received any call from Sally yesterday. We then think that Edward went to the cliffs and waited for your boat to pass by. Then he returned the rifle to the storage shed behind the general store where he had been keeping it and his other guns for years."

"For years?" Sophie asked.

"Yeah, since he was a boy."

"And no one ever found them, knew about them?" I asked incredulously.

"Everyone knew about them. Everyone but Edward's mother, that is. You see, Edward's father taught him to use guns for hunting and target practice on his visits there. As the years went by, he grew to be an excellent marksman and won a number of junior championships in Washington State."

Sophie and I glanced at each other but said nothing. We listened to Robby's narration in rapt silence. "Mrs. Magill hated guns and forbade Edward to use them. But he wouldn't give them up. So in his summers in Havenport he practiced in secret. One reason he loved shooting so much was that it was just about the only bond he had with his dad. Mr. Magill managed to have a number of them shipped here to Havenport and convinced the Wrights to allow them to be stored in their shed. Edward was always so responsible and careful with them, and he only used them for target practice that there was never any problem. He even was a member of the shooting club at Yale and never let his mother know about that."

I nodded. I had always been surprised that Yale and a number of other Ivy League schools had shooting clubs, but they had been around for years.

"Edward enjoyed teaching me to use the rifle, and I became a halfway decent shot by the time I joined the police force. But I never was anywhere near as good as Edward. One of his rifles that he secretly kept here was a special one that his father gave him on his eighteenth birthday. It was very expensive and rather unusual. It meant a lot to Edward. He always spent a great amount of time cleaning and maintaining it. I won't go into any technical detail, but it required a type of ammo that's not used much around here. One of those bullets . . ."

"Killed Tom Wright?" I finished for him.

"Yeah. When I got this information this morning, I went to the storage shed and found all Edward's equipment missing. I guess he had second thoughts about leaving that rifle back in the shed. He took them all out last night. You saw him bury them, Mr. Hunt. When I then went to the Magill house to continue our discussion, my mother told me you two had left the house with the folding shovels Edward and I had used when we went camping as kids. When I saw Mrs. Magill's car parked on the harbor road, I went looking for you."

"And you found us, Robby," I said softly. "Was the rifle that used the unusual bullets one of the ones buried?"

"Yes, it was. But from what you say it had been there over night. I wasn't able to tell if it had recently been fired."

"I take it," I was heartsick as I went on, "that if you had had possession of the rifle earlier you might have been able to make that determination. Is that correct?"

"I might have been able to, yes."

"I see, Robby." No one spoke for a moment or two, but it was clear that everyone could hear the sadness in my voice and read the guilt in my eyes.

"Mr. Hunt, I won't pull any punches with you. Your interference has delayed our investigation in this case. Now I could very easily pull you both in for obstructing justice or concealing evidence or some such thing. But I'm not gonna do that. I know you both meant well and wanted to help. But you haven't helped, Mr. Hunt. Just the opposite."

I was not able to look at Sophie. I didn't need to. I knew she was as upset as I was. She must be. I forced myself to face Robby as he said, "I'd sure have every right to ask you both to leave the village as soon as possible. But I don't have to, do I? I'm sure you won't get in the way of the investigation any more. And I heard that you're going to put together some sort of a memorial tribute to Tom with the Little

Players. Right? I think that will be a good thing for the town and for Barbara Wright. So go right ahead and do that. All right, Mr. Hunt?"

"Yes, Robby. Thank you."

"I know you'll do a good job. Well, come on now, you two. I'll drive you back to your car."

"No thank you, Patrolman Donohue." I was startled to hear Sophie's voice. "It's almost noon, and we told Barbara Wright we would meet her in the old church. It's only a short walk from here."

"Okay, if that's what you want," Robby said. "You two take care now."

We remained sitting as we heard Robby leave the station and start his car.

"Bull crap!"

I swiveled my head around so fast when Sophie said these two surprising words that my skull ached even more than usual.

"Double dipped bull crap!" she elaborated. "There's more to this whole thing than the tidy little story Robby just spun for us."

I looked at Sophie with amazement. "Like any cop," she continued, "he wants this mess all neatly explained, wrapped up with a pink ribbon, put away and forgotten. And with Edward out of the picture and probably not with the living for too much longer, Robby and the state police all have an easy, obvious culprit. But it's too easy, and too tidy, and there are still those messy little nagging details that Robby refused to acknowledge or even consider. We promised Madge that we would find out the truth. I'm not at all sure we have it yet, at least not all of it. I say we continue searching for it: the truth, the whole truth and nothing but the truth . . ."

"So help us, God's deputy," I finished for her. I amazed myself. I had never thought I would smile again.

Chapter 17

"While you're settling in, Mr. Hunt, I'm sure you'll be tickled pink to know how absolutely lucky you are not to have had your nasty little trauma before 1972 when all they had available to them were only poor little X-rays to image your big old head. And I'm sure you realize, Mr. Hunt, that having only that technique to use they were only ever able to show the bones of the skull and could not, no matter how absolutely hard they tried, they could not distinguish any of the details of your big old brain. Given this absolutely major limitation, the medical world was absolutely stunned in '72 when, get this, Mr. Hunt, a neurologist and an engineer from EMI, you know, the same British company that produced the Beatles' records, isn't that remarkable, Mr. Hunt? Well, the medical world was just flabbergasted when those gentlemen presented their absolutely spanking brand new technique called computerized tomography or CT. I know you're absolutely tickled pink to learn this, aren't you, Mr. Hunt? This absolutely incredible advance over regular computer imaging allowed, for absolutely the very first time, different parts of your big old brain including the ventricles, you know those fluid-filled spaces . . . Yes, that's right, Mr. Hunt, you just lie right down there on that table, that's right . . . well, those cute little ventricles of yours could now, for absolutely the very first time, be imaged distinctly as well as could the gray and the white matter of your big old brain, Mr. Hunt, and they all could be shown as thin little brain slices on the computer, absolutely thin as thin could be . . . Are you comfy now, Mr. Hunt.? You're going to be taking an absolutely fabulous little trip into that big doughnut hole in that machine behind you . . . And I know you're going to be tickled pink to learn that over the years CT has undergone absolutely tremendous progress. Originally the scan time took a good hour, could you believe that, Mr. Hunt? The scan used to take a good hour to complete. Can you imagine trying not to move for that length of time, can you, Mr. Hunt? What's more, the images that were then produced were pretty coarse, I blush to admit. But nowadays, Mr. Hunt, nowadays, you'll be tickled pink to discover that the same scan can be done in a little bitty fraction of that time, and the produced images are absolutely much, much sharper. Now, let me make just an absolutely teensy-weensy adjustment to your cute little head there, Mr. Hunt, and we'll be just about ready to proceed. I know you'll be tickled pink to get this absolutely fabulous little trip into that big old doughnut under way. Won't you, Mr. Hunt? Mr. Hunt? Mr. Huuunt . . ."

I stopped myself from listening to the over-enthusiastic, more than slightly manic radiologist with the irritatingly syrupy voice and limited vocabulary. I desperately tried to direct my thoughts away from what the damned *absolutely stunning computerized tomography* might soon frighteningly reveal about my goddamn *cute-little-fluid-filled-ventricles*. Instead, I directed my thoughts back to all that had happened in the past few hours to turn my life literally upside down.

Fueled by Sophie's optimistic and enthusiastic war cry to continue our investigation despite Robby's admonitions not to, we decided that we should take this opportunity to move full speed ahead before the patrolman had a chance to squelch our work further. So, we would leave the police station in two separate directions. I would walk the short distance to the church where Barbara Wright apparently awaited me. Sophie would walk down the shoreline the half mile or so to the Benson house where she would question Noah Benson about his trip to and from the airport. She would then continue along the Harbor Road the short distance to where we had left Madge's car and then drive to the church where she would pick me up.

As I rose from the chair in the police station, I felt a little light headed but assured myself it was only the adrenalin rush that would naturally accompany my decision to continue the hunt. I bade Sophie *a bientot* at the door and watched her vigorously take a sharp right till she was out of sight. The sky had darkened considerably since we had entered the station, and the wind was blowing even more briskly now. I buttoned my jacket completely and turned up the collar as I began to walk the two and a half deserted blocks to the churchyard. As I crossed the second street corner, I must have missed my step somehow and strangely tripped and fell like a lummox into the middle of the street suddenly facing two oncoming headlights accompanied by the cacophony of screeching brakes and a blaring horn. In that split second I glimpsed three pairs of eyes staring wide-eyed at me from the van's front seat. I noticed one pair of eyes was blue; one pair was brown, and the third pair had one of each color. What the devil? I thought as I passed out.

I must have blacked out for less than a minute, but it was enough time for the owners of those eyes to alight from the van and bend over my inert body lying on the street. When I awoke a light beam was probing my left eye. The small flashlight resembled the one Sophie had given me when I followed Edward on the beach last night. The hand holding the penlight was not Sophie's however. It belonged to one of the most attractive women I have ever seen. Even in my beclouded, discombobulated state I couldn't miss that. Her striking pale blue eyes showed kind concern, concern for me. Her perfectly formed, lusciously full lips opened. It took a second or two for me to realize that those lips were speaking, speaking to me.

"I'm sorry. I'm afraid I missed that," I babbled. Those lips then miraculously assembled themselves into the most captivating smile I had ever remembered seeing.

"I asked," those mesmerizing lips repeated, "how are you feeling?"

As I started to lift my head off the ground, the lips spoke again. "Whoa, just lie back while I examine you a little more, all right?"

How could I deny those lips anything? I lay back on the street. As she shone the light on my other eye and efficiently yet gently ran her tapered fingers over my head and neck, I noticed that she was dressed in a lab coat.

"Doctor?" I brilliantly deduced.

"Yes, Dr. Rodgers, how do you do? And you are Harrison Hunt, are you not? I've seen you around the village. How are you feeling, Mr. Hunt?"

"I'm feeling a lot better now, Doctor." I immediately turned scarlet as I finally came to my senses and realized how ridiculous I must sound to this vision before me.

"I'm glad to hear that, Mr. Hunt. Can you tell me what happened?"

"I seem to have fainted . . . again." Before I could continue, I heard a deep male voice to the doctor's left say, "We're creating a traffic jam, you know."

Another car had stopped behind the doctor's van unable to move because of the obstruction we were causing in the street. Asking her companion to assist her, the two of them gingerly helped me to my feet and into the back seat of the van. The doctor sat next to me; the man with the deep voice opened the front door and sat in the driver's seat next to a good-sized mostly white dog who had been patiently waiting in the van all this time. The dog looked at me curiously and I observed that the two differently colored eyes I had briefly noticed belonged to him. He seemed also somehow to be genuinely concerned about my well being as concerned as was the doctor, or was I imagining things?

"You said this wasn't the first time you fainted, Mr. Hunt?"

I turned my attention back to the attractive Dr. Rodgers and related (in a very edited fashion) how I had passed out on the beach last night and then again a few minutes ago on the street.

"And when did you receive this alarming bump on your head?"

"Last night. I must have hit my head when I collapsed. It's caused me quite a headache."

"So you fell backwards on the beach?"

"No, straight forward on my face. Not very graceful I'm afraid."

"Then how did you manage to get such a severe bruise on the back of your head? It certainly looks like something hit you from behind, very forcibly."

"But that's impossible," I stammered. "There was no one behind me when I blacked out last night."

"Do you think you may have forgotten some of what happened? It's not uncommon in cases of concussion to have memory lapses."

"Concussion?" I gasped.

"Mr. Hunt, how long have you had aniscoria?"

"Anise what?" I didn't know what she was talking about.

"Aniscoria is the medical term for unequal pupil size." My look of incomprehension prompted her to continue. "The pupil is the black part in the center of the eye. It gets larger in dim light and smaller in bright light. Your right pupil, Mr. Hunt, is larger than your left. Here look for yourself."

Looking at my eyes in the small mirror she held out to me, I could see a slight difference in the size of my two pupils. A difference I had never noticed before. I told that to her.

"Small differences in pupil sizes are found in up to one in five healthy people. Babies born with different sized pupils may not have any underlying disorder. There are a number of well known people who function very well with aniscoria. David Bowie is a case in point . . ."

"Uh oh. There's an 'on the other hand' just itching to pop out here, isn't there?" I interrupted. That delicious warm smile of hers appeared again. "I'm afraid you're right, Mr. Hunt. Your aniscoria may be of no medical concern whatsoever. *On the other hand,* it may be a result of bleeding inside your skull caused by a severe injury."

"And that could be serious, couldn't it, doctor?"

"To find out one way or the other I strongly suggest that you have a scan done. I run a small medical center not too far away. In fact, I'll be going there shortly. I believe I can schedule an appointment for you this afternoon. The sooner we have the results, the better we'll be able to proceed. Shall I make that appointment for you, Mr. Hunt?"

"It would seem I have no choice."

"Good. Please give me your phone number, and I'll call you with the appointment time and the exact address of the center."

Her smile was infectious. I gave her the information and told her that I believed Sophie and I had passed the medical center returning from the airport early this morning. She asked if she could drive me home now, and I requested instead a short hop to the church where Barbara Wright must be wondering where I was.

"Basil, would you be so kind as to drop Mr. Hunt off at the old church?" I sensed a more formal tone in her voice when she addressed the deep-voiced man. His response was a dismissive grunt. I think I did not like this Basil. But that was irrelevant. Although suddenly very concerned and uncertain about my health, I was certain of one thing: I was happy I had run into Dr. Rodgers. Pun intended

Chapter 18

"Now, don't you be concerned about that itsy bitsy noise you must be hearing as you're riding back through that big old, cute old doughnut, Mr. Hunt. You're not to worry your cute old picture-perfect grey cells about that, if you don't mind my rakish bit of wit, Mr. Hunt, Mr. Hunt. Mr. Huuuunt . . . ."

As I endeavored to drown out the radiologist's insipid banter I concentrated on remembering what transpired when I was let off at the church. I had been there before. Madge had given us a tour of the building on a happier day. The village and all its historic buildings were very important to Madge, but the old stone church was obviously her favorite. She told us it was built in 1697 and was the second oldest extant church and the fifteenth oldest extant building in the state. I remember her particularly commenting on its two-foot-thick fieldstone walls that gave way to clapboard above the roofline. I now looked up at the west end of the roof at the octagonal wooden open belfry. The three of us had climbed to the belfry two weeks ago. Within it was the original bell. Madge read aloud its engraved Biblical verse and then translated the Latin: "If God be for us, who can be against us." Maybe I could understand how the stress of recent events had brought Madge's spiritual inclinations to the forefront. Maybe that was why I became God's deputy in her mind.

Perhaps it was a gust of cold wind that caused me to shiver right then or maybe it was something else. In any case, I crossed through the well-kept though slightly creepy graveyard. A few shrubs flanked the stone steps that led up to the main entrance: paneled wooden double doors recessed within a Gothic archway. I entered the church looking for a second woman whose heart, like Madge's, was full of sorrow. I saw no one. The silence of the church's interior was tangible. Where was Barbara? I softly walked down the center aisle past the wooden pews which faced the raised pulpit.

I nearly jumped out of my skin. Deafening chords swept through the church like the flapping wings of an avenging angel. Regaining my breath, I climbed the short spiral stair to the enclosed choir loft. There was Barbara Wright seated at the pipe organ attacking the keys with all the ferocity she could muster.

Her back was towards me, so I couldn't see the expression on her face. But the suffering she must be feeling clearly evidenced itself in the stiffness in her back and neck muscles as well as in the violent way her fingers struck the keys. I didn't know what I should say or even if I should make my presence known to her at all. Would she be embarrassed, ashamed, or even angry to know that I had been a witness to her expression of such violent emotion?

I quickly decided that discretion should be the better part of valor and silently descended the staircase. My hurriedly conceived plan was to call her cell phone with mine to tell her I was a block or two from the church and would be there soon and also apologize for my lateness. That way she would never know I had been up in the choir loft.

The dissonant, agonized chords continued as I retraced my steps back through the church. But just as I neared the front doors, lo and behold my damned cell phone started to ring. It would of course decide on this particular opportunity to at last snag a signal! The Fifth Brandenburg Concerto reverberated through the edifice jubilantly revealing my presence there. Barbara immediately stopped playing.

I had no choice but to retrieve my cell phone with as much clumsy speed as I could and pick up the call. It was Dr. Rodgers advising me that I could be seen at the medical center at 3:00 pm. Would that do? I responded that it would and thanked her. I would have preferred to converse with her longer, but the awkwardness of the situation forced me to cut the call short. Talk about lousy timing. Now Barbara would know that I must have overheard her.

All I could do now was clutch at the flimsiest of straws. "Barbara," I called loudly from the front of the church, "Barbara, are you there?" I paused a few seconds then shouted out once again, "Barbara? Are you still here? It's Harrison Hunt." I held my breath and crossed my fingers.

After another pause I heard, "Harry? Yes, I'm here. I'll be right down." Her voice quivered a bit as she spoke."

It sounded as if she then blew her nose, and soon I watched her slowly come down the spiral staircase and shakily sit down in the first row of pews. I walked up to her and sat down beside her. "Hello, Barbara," was all I could say observing how fragile she looked sitting there.

"Hello, Harry. Thank you for meeting with me. I thought you might not show up."

"Barbara, I'm so sorry I'm late. I had a little accident, but I'm here now. Sophie should be here shortly."

"Actually, it was you I wanted to see, Harry. There are two requests I would like to ask you."

Oh no, Two more damned requests to add to the list! That's what I wanted to say but looking at her red-rimmed, grief-filled eyes I of course said, "Whatever I'm able to do for you, Barbara, of course I'll do."

"Thank you, Harry. The first shouldn't be too difficult for you. I heard that you're putting together a little memorial for Tom at Laurence House."

"That's right. I'll be working with the Little Players on some additional Shakespearean texts that I hope will be a fitting tribute. I'll be distributing the sides tonight. The rehearsals will be held each evening for a presentation on Thursday."

"Well, Harry, I want to be a part of the program. It will help me take my mind off . . . things."

I was a little surprised. "Are you sure, Barbara?"

"I'm sure." The look she gave me was so concentrated and fierce that it rather took be aback. I of course concurred and asked her if she would feel more comfortable if she were partnered with Robby Donohue once again. Their scene yesterday (Was it really only yesterday?) had gone very well.

"No," she said with that same quite fierce gleam in her eye. "I would prefer to do a piece alone. One that would be a personal statement from me to my husband and . . . . my daughter." Her eyes filled with tears. Mine did too.

I started to offer her some encouraging words but she quickly interrupted me. "This leads me to my second request, which I'm afraid will be more difficult for you to grant. I ran into poor Madge Magill at the hospital this morning. You know her son is still in very critical condition. She told me how happy you made her by agreeing to find out the truth of all that has happened. She believes that Edward was not to blame for Tom's death or for whatever has happened to Sally. She believes you will uncover evidence of some sort to prove his innocence. I am afraid I am not as confident as Madge is of this. But I want you also to help me. I want you to discover where Sally is and what has happened to her. All my calls to her friends proved fruitless. If someone has hurt my little girl, even if it turns out to be Edward, I need you to find out his identify so the bastard can be killed!" Her voice rose in pitch and volume as she spat out these words, and the tension in her body returned in spades. "Promise me you'll catch him, Harry. Promise me!" she almost screamed.

What could I say? No words came out of my mouth. I could only nod my head and hold Barbara Wright's hand. She nodded as well. Her voice was now much more relaxed and lower in tone. "Thank you. Now that I've carried out the two bits of business I had to do today: working out the details of Tom's funeral with Reverend Pembroke this morning and now seeing to it that justice will be done, I would like to show you something."

I gulped but quietly followed her out the church and into the graveyard. The way she walked and carried herself now made me think that this was a woman with a mission, a mission that must be completed.

"This is the peaceful spot where Tom will rest," Barbara said softly, "among the other Wrights." Indeed I could read the names of many of their ancestors on the nearby tombstones. "I have also asked the reverend to make this a double plot as well." She looked at me. "For Sally, if need be, when you find her." I gulped once more.

Saved by the bell, I said silently to myself as my cell phone rang again. This time it was Sophie who told me she was now on her way in Madge's car to the church with, as she put it, "some interesting news." I told her I had quite a bit of news to impart to her as well.

Barbara was now on her knees bent over the plot of land picking weeds and smoothing the ground with her hands. She did not seem to hear me when I told her Sophie would be here in a few minutes. She did not seem to hear me when I asked if we could give her a lift. She did not seem to hear me when I said goodbye, see you at Laurence House at 6:00. She did not seem to hear me get into the car.

"Should I go over to talk to Barbara before we leave?" Sophie asked me looking with concern at the kneeling figure.

"I think she has all the company she wants right now," I said softly.

Chapter

19

"Last stop! Last stop on the old doughnut express. Everybody off! That means little old you, Mr. Hunt. Your fun-packed voyage through the wonders of CT technology is now complete. Let me help move your cute big old body up to a sitting position. There you are, honey lamb. That wasn't so bad was it? No siree, Bob. It was a fun-packed trip, wasn't it, Mr. Hunt? Mr. Hunt? Mr. Huuuuunt . . ."

As the unrivalled winner of the Radiologist You'd Most Like to Strangle Award babbled on and on while advising me to have a seat and relax after the thrill of the *old doughnut choo-choo,* to maintain my sanity I continued focusing my thoughts on all that transpired during the last two hours.

Sophie parked a block from the church and listened with rapt attention to what I described of my meeting with Barbara. "Poor Barbara. She really flipped out then, Harry?"

"You should have seen (and heard) her performance at the organ and then the look in her eyes as she cast me in my next role," I remarked with a grimace.

"So now, boss, you're not only God's deputy but a member of the, what, Justice League of America?" Sophie chuckled and rolled her eyes.

"The Justice League?" I didn't get her reference.

"Oh, you know, Harry. That team of Super-heroes from the comic books. So who would you best represent? Superman? Batman? The Green Hornet?"

"Very amusing, Sophie . . ."

"No, I don't think tights and spandex are really you. The Flash? Wonder Woman? No, I doubt your expertise with her lasso of truth. Or maybe . . ."

The look I threw Sophie caused her laughter to dissipate. "Sorry, boss. You know how much I empathize with Barbara and what she's going through, but you must admit these conflicting quests you're now committed to pursue are pretty bizarre."

To show Sophie how well I understood the ludicrousness of my situation, I responded with a slight smile and one of her own favorite expressions, "When you're right, you're right."

After a brief moment of silence, I could see that a new thought had occurred to her. "You said you were late arriving at the church, Harry. Did something delay you?"

I turned away from Sophie and stared straight ahead out the windshield and watched the nearby trees swaying in the wind. My expression must have been strange enough to cause her to worry. "What happened, Harry?"

I took a deep breath then told her everything that had happened beginning with my passing out in the street and ending with my upcoming appointment at 3:00 at the medical center for some sort of a head scan. I concluded with, "I must admit, Sophie, you've been correct all along. I was remiss in not seeing a doctor as soon as I collapsed the first time at the beach."

Instead of gloating at this opportunity to say 'I told you so,' Sophie simply reached over, took my hand and squeezed it. Have I mentioned how lucky I am to have Sophie in my life?

"Well, I'm not going to accomplish anything sitting around here feeling sorry for myself. You haven't told me what you learned at the Benson house. You said you had some interesting news?"

"Yes, I do," Sophie replied, "but not from the Bensons. No one was home and their car was not in the driveway."

"Bummer!" I piped up quickly and then added, "Now where did I learn that colorful expostulation? Oh yes, I know . . ." I paused as I remembered that it was Sally who always delighted in using that expression. Sophie and I looked at each other silently for a moment.

Then she continued, "I started walking to where we left the car and I spied Noah Benson's limousine parked at the wharf near where he keeps the charter boats he rents out. The car was locked and the slip reserved for one of the boats was empty. I assume he had taken a party out on a fishing or sightseeing expedition. But, listen to this. When I looked into the limo I saw that there was one of those microphones on the dashboard next to the driver's seat that limo drivers use to communicate with their dispatcher. I suddenly remembered that Noah had used it to call in when he drove us to Havenport from the railroad station on our first day here."

"You know, I believe I remember that too, Sophie. So why then didn't Nora suggest that we use that to talk to her husband when Edward was his passenger."

"Right," Sophie agreed. "She just told us about his forgotten cell phone. Nothing about her ability to contact him by radio."

"Very strange, Sophie, very strange. We definitely have many questions to put to the Bensons. We should see them tonight at the rehearsal."

"I'll look forward to that. And speaking of cell phones, when I got back in the car I decided to examine the cell phone that mysteriously appeared in your jacket pocket this morning. I had plugged it in Madge's car charger and it now was fully charged."

"Oh good. Whose phone is it, and how did I happen to obtain it?"

"Here, let's look at it together." She reached in her tote bag, retrieved the phone and turned it on. "I was afraid it might be password protected, which is an option you can choose on a cell phone." I made a sound to indicate the surprise I felt to learn this. "But, fortunately," she continued, "it wasn't locked." The phone sprang to life and a photograph appeared on the faceplate. I gasped. It was a picture of Edward in a jacket and tie and Sally also all dressed up. They were grinning from ear to ear and each held a flute glass filled with something bubbly. They were apparently celebrating some happy moment in a nice restaurant, cocktail lounge, or the like. "I located the date stamp for this photo," Sophie said grimly. "Get ready for this, Harry. It was taken last evening at the time Edward told us he and Sally were at the movies."

"Zounds, Sophie. So Edward is a liar, at least he lied about where he and Sally went last night. So they obviously didn't have a fight at the movie theatre after the film and she obviously didn't go off from the theatre with a girl friend."

"Let's see if we can find out some more information about that. If I'm recalling correctly, the medical center is in the same little mall where the cineplex is located."

"Yes, I think you're right." I looked at my watch. "We have some time before my appointment. Let's go see what we can discover at the movie theatre."

Sophie started the car and typed the address Dr. Rodgers had provided for the medical center on the GPS. The crisp, unflappable voice of Manderville began politely but efficiently to provide the turn by turn directions as we drove a few minutes in silence lost in our thoughts.

Suddenly, I asked, "So whose phone is it that we've just looked at? It's not Sally's, right, because we've inferred that hers was broken and found by Robby in her bedroom. And she only had one, at least according to Edward, the veracity of whom is becoming more and more dubious."

"No, it doesn't appear to be Sally's phone. I poked around at the other photographs remaining on the phone as well as the phone's address book, and I'm pretty sure I know whose phone it is. Look at the number that comes up when you touch the entry labeled 'Mom' on the quick dial list. "Do you recognize that number?"

I looked at the phone number that appeared. "O gods and goddesses!" I cried out voicing a favorite oath from *Cymbeline*. That's the Magill home phone number. This must be Edward's phone. How did it get in my jacket pocket?"

"Let's worry about that a little later, boss, what do you say? We have quite a bit on our plates right now, don't you think?"

I agreed and we were mostly silent as we drove to the shopping mall. I noticed that we were actually reversing our route from the airport. It was 2:45 pm when Manderville advised us we had reached our destination. There were a few vehicles parked in front of the medical center including Dr. Rodgers' van. We then drove to the other end of the mall and parked as near to the movies as we could. The Sunday matinee must still be playing as there were many more cars parked at this end.

We walked up to the ticket booth. I asked the young woman inside what time the show ended. She told us in twenty minutes.

"So the 7:00 pm screening last night would have gotten out at about 9:05, is that right?

"9:08," she answered matter-of-factly.

"You wouldn't have happened to be on duty last night by any chance, were you?"

She looked at me more intently. "Yes, I was. Why?"

"As it happens," I replied, "two young friends of ours might have been at the movie last night. We were told that they had some sort of disagreement outside the theatre after the film ended."

What she then said absolutely took me by surprise. "If you mean Edward Magill and Sally Wright, your information is correct, sir."

"You mean you saw them here around 9:08?" Sophie asked. "Are you sure?"

"Yes, ma'am, I am. I've known Sally all my life and I know Edward as well. I was a little surprised to see them have a few words last night right in front of my booth. But I guess lovers' spats aren't all that unusual, are they?"

"Did Sally leave with Edward, do you recall?"

"No sir, I saw Sally call someone on her phone and then tell Edward to go on home alone as her friend would be coming to pick her up."

"Was that her pretty pink sparkly phone?" Sophie asked.

"Yes it was. She always used that funny little phone."

"Did you see who this friend was who picked her up?"

"No, ma'am. Ticket buyers for the 9:30 show started to come then and I was too busy to notice when Sally left. Sorry, ma'am."

"Harry, it's almost 3:00. We better leave. Thank you very much for your help, uh . . ."

"I'm Roxanne Willis. You're welcome."

As we crossed the small shopping mall, I said, "I just don't understand any of this. How could they have been seen here in front of the theatre if they were busy toasting each other with champagne somewhere else at the same time? That time stamp said 9:02, didn't it, Sophie?"

"It did indeed, boss. And what about her phone? I need to write this down and go over all my notes."

I told her to do just that as we entered the small medical center. The first person I saw was the deep-voiced man from Dr. Rodgers' van. I walked over to him and held out my hand.

"Hello, I'm Harrison Hunt and I believe I'm here for . . ."

"I know who you are," he rudely interrupted, "and you're late. Follow me. This way." He briskly led me to a door at the end of a corridor, opened it and waited for me to enter.

"Uh, Sophie . . ." I started to say.

"She can sit in the waiting room over there," he pointed and then quickly walked away.

"Nice friendly people around here," Sophie said with an edge. "You go, Harry. I'll wait in there for you. And Harry," she added sincerely, "break a leg."

Chapter 20

"Mr. Hunt? Mr. Hunt? Mr. Hunt?"

I continued trying to shut out that irritating sound from my consciousness, but somehow I became aware the voice had altered. I opened my eyes and was delighted to find that the radiologist from hell had morphed into Doctor Quinn, Medicine Woman. Well, she wasn't an exact ringer for Jane Seymour in that TV Western from the '90s, but Dr. Rodgers was without doubt an attractive woman and a pleasure now to see. I donned my most debonair demeanor and with my most devilish delivery wittily came up with, "What's up, doc?"

If the lovely lady doctor was at all disappointed with this *bon mot* as she certainly might have been, she didn't reveal a bit of it. "You seem to have survived the scan in fine fettle, Mr. Hunt. How are you feeling now? Is your headache still bothering you?"

"I'm afraid it wasn't helped by the non-stop narration from the conductor of *that little old doughnut express,*" I said with a slight laugh.

The laugh was picked up by Dr. Rodgers. "Oh, Janice can be a bit overenthusiastic at times, but she's very good at her job."

"I daresay she is. So, how long will it take for you to make a diagnosis?"

"It will take a little while, but I do have two more patients to see first. Why don't you join your friend in the waiting room for now. I'll see you as soon as I can." Those delectable lips forming that scrumptious smile again. How could I demur?

Redoubtable Sophie was engrossed in her notebook when I sat down beside her. "Working hard?" I asked her.

"Never a rest for the weary," she said with an exaggerated sigh. Then, "How did it go, Harry?"

"Except for an especially irritating technician not too badly really. The doctor said she would get back to us with the results as soon as possible, but it might take some time. In the meanwhile, I can only wish that you have solved all our mysteries by simply poring over your inestimable notes."

"As your pal Shakespeare said: 'If wishes were horses . . .'"

"Would you believe it, Sophie, although it does originate in the 16th century, this bit of wisdom is not by the immortal Bard. It's actually the beginning of an old Scottish proverb or nursery rhyme. Let's see if I can remember the whole thing.

> If wishes were horses then beggars would ride.
>
> If turnips were swords I'd have one by my side.
>
> If 'ifs' and 'ands' were pots and pans
>
> There would be no need for tinker's hands.

Well, who says that my bump on the head might have caused memory losses?"

"Not I, boss, that's for sure," Sophie declared with a smile. "Well, I definitely agree with that proverb. Results more often are achieved through action than through wishing. And actively reading over and over from my notes what little Miss ticket-seller Roxanne Willis told us has brought up some questions in my mind."

"Has it indeed? So there's something fishy in what she told us?"

Nodding, Sophie said, "I think I wrote down pretty much what she said *verbatim*. First of all, when she told us that Edward and Sally had a 'lover's spat,' she said that they had, and I quote, '*a few words*.' In checking my notes, that is exactly how Edward described their little squabble when Robby Donohue questioned him in the Wrights' apartment. See," she showed me the relevant page of her notes:

> Robby: You left her at the movies? Why was that, Edward?
>
> Edward: Well, I don't really see why it's any of your business, but we had what I guess you could call a few words after the film ended, and Sally told me she'd rather not go home with me. She said she'd get one of her girl friends to pick her up. I waited while she made a call on her cell, and when she had arranged the ride home I drove off.

"Also, boss, did you notice how polite Roxanne became after she knew we were interested in Edward and Sally's whereabouts last night? She suddenly addressed us as 'sir' and 'ma'am' which she hadn't when she first talked to us."

"In just the same way the polite 'you' is employed in Shakespearean text rather than the informal 'thou.'"

"Exactly. And who has always been the most polite person you could think of?"

"Edward Magill, without a doubt. So you think Edward coached Roxanne on her story? That's rather circumstantial evidence, don't you think?"

"I agree with you, Harry. If that were all I had. However," she added with excitement, "It's a simple procedure to access to whom Edward texted messages last evening from his phone. After he went to his bedroom and before he sneaked off to the Wrights' shed for the guns, he sent a text."

She showed me the relevant entry on Edward's phone. It read: '11:14 pm. Roxanne'

"WE NEED TO FIND OUT the truth about this, Sophie."

"I absolutely agree, boss." And with a determined press of a button, she dialed the number identified as 'Roxanne' on Edward's phone and put the call on speakerphone. It rang. And rang again. And . . .

"Oh my God!" the startled voice screamed. "Edward, is that you? I heard you were practically dead. Is that really you?"

"No, Ms. Willis, I'm afraid this is not Edward. I'm using his phone. I'm sorry I frightened you when you saw his name pop up as the caller. This is Sophie Xerxes. Harrison Hunt and I asked you some questions about Edward and Sally a little while ago."

There was no response. "Roxanne, are you still there?"

"Yes, I'm still here." The girl's voice was more subdued now. "What can I do for you, ma'am?"

"Mr. Hunt and I have a few more questions to ask you if you don't mind. We'd like to come back to the theatre now to speak to you. If you don't mind?"

"No, I don't mind at all, ma'am. But I'm not there right now. I'm on my dinner break. I'll be back in an hour and would be only too glad to speak to you then."

I whispered to Sophie, "Let's get to her now before she has time to think up another good story."

"We're on a rather tight schedule, Roxanne. How about we join you for dinner. Our treat." Sophie smiled at my disdainful reaction to her offer. "Where can we find you?"

Roxanne seemed to have no choice but to tell us she was at a little place located almost directly behind the cineplex. Telling her we would be right there, Sophie hung up.

"Sophie, I have to let Dr. Rodgers know that I'll be away for a bit before I leave." I was rising from my chair to do this when, speak of the devil, (or rather its opposite) the doctor quickly entered the waiting room and said to me, "I'm so sorry, Mr. Hunt . . ."

In that fraction of a second, I blanched and almost had a heart attack. What terrible news was she about to tell me? Did I have brain injury? Was I about to die? What?

Then she finished her sentence: "I'm so sorry, Mr. Hunt, but I have to go out on an emergency call. I won't be able to get back here to evaluate your results until after the center closes at 5 o'clock. I know how important this is to you. Let me think. You're staying at the Magill home, right? That's only a few minutes from where I live. Would you mind coming by my place this evening? We can then take all the time we'll need to discuss your condition."

"Thank you, that is very considerate of you, doctor. But I have a rehearsal for the memorial for Tom Wright this evening. I don't think it will be over until 8 or 9."

"That's perfectly all right, Mr. Hunt. Come over when you're finished. I'm really a night owl. Here's my card." Quickly saying goodbye to Sophie and me she rushed out the door followed immediately by the rather rude Basil (who didn't give either of us a second glance) and surprisingly by the handsome white dog I had seen in the van. He certainly gave me a cordial look as he followed the others out of the building.

As Sophie and I walked behind the movie theatre, we easily spotted the restaurant and were surprised to discover that it was another Cousin Carrie's Home Style Cooking, the third one we've come across. This was the smallest we've seen so far. But there was a drive-through line on the side of the building that seemed to be doing good business. "Cousin Carrie must be rolling in the chips, and I don't mean French fries," I remarked. The interior décor was similar to the branch at the airport. I noticed the laminated poster of the three-month old restaurant review once again prominently displayed by the front register. There were several customers seated at the pine counter, but only Roxanne was occupying a booth. We joined her and sat down.

"Thank you for seeing us, Roxanne," Sophie said with a smile. Roxanne nodded but seemed a little more nervous than she had appeared before. "Roxanne, you said you were friends with both Sally and Edward. Well, so are we. We're trying to help both of them, and we think you want to help them too."

"I do want to help them," Roxanne's lower lip started to quiver.

I took over the questioning, "Then you have to tell us the truth. Lies won't help us find Sally. Lies won't help us prove that Edward did not do something terrible." Tears were filling Roxanne's eyes now. "Did you really see the two of them at the movies last night or did Edward ask you to say that?"

Sophie took hold of Roxanne's hands. "If Edward is your friend, please tell us the truth so we can find out what really happened and help him. Please, Roxanne."

That did it. The dam burst, and the poor girl started to sob. "I only wanted to help Edward. I've loved him since I first met him. But he only had eyes for Sally. I was cool with that. If Edward was happy, then I was happy too. So when he came by and asked me to say, if anyone inquired, that he and Sally were at the show, of course I said I would."

I was not entirely clear what she meant. "When did he come by and ask you that?"

"Yesterday afternoon. He said Sally wanted him to take her to someplace her parents wouldn't approve, so they told them they were just going to the movies. I promised him I would confirm that if anyone asked."

"But Edward texted you later that evening," Sophie probed.

"Yes, he said something had happened and I was to add to the story what I told you."

"That you saw them have an argument and that they left separately?"

"Yes," she wept. "I promised. I would promise him anything. I don't know what really happened, I don't know where they really went last night, but I know Edward would never hurt anyone. I trust him. I love him. And now he's probably going to die, and I'll never have the chance to tell him. And people will always think that he did something bad to Sally. But I know he didn't. I just know it."

Looking at the poor distraught girl, my heart went out to her. "We're better able to find out what really happened now that you've told us the truth. I know Edward would thank you for that if he could."

Sophie patted her hand and said, "Now, why don't you go back to work, wash your face and put on some fresh makeup. You'll feel much better. We'll take care of your check, and we'll let you know anything we find out that will help exonerate Edward."

"You promise?"

"Yes, we promise. You can trust us the way Edward trusted you."

Roxanne smiled a bit at Sophie. We remained in the booth after she left. Neither of us could say anything for a few minutes. Then I leaned my head back and expelled the longest, loudest sigh of my life.

"Well, this has certainly been some day."

"One for the record books," said Sophie. "And it's not over yet. We still have to put together the texts for the memorial, get through the first rehearsal and then . . ." She looked at me.

"And then receive my death decree from the doctor!"

Although I had delivered the last line in my most melodramatic, over-the-top manner and punctuated it with a jovial laugh, I knew Sophie didn't buy it. She knew how worried I really was. "We'll take each thing as it comes, one step at a time. As we always have," she said quietly. Have I told you how grateful I am that Sophie is in my life?

"And I think the first thing we should do is have something to eat. It seems like a year since we've eaten." As we sampled Cousin Carrie's cuisine, (The New England style clam chowder and lobster rolls were actually quite good.) we prepared the material for the rehearsal to our satisfaction and deposited it all back inside the confines of Sophie's spacious and irreplaceable tote bag.

On the drive back to Laurence House, I mused that it would seem necessary for us to find out where exactly Sally and Edward did go last night. Roxanne said she didn't know, and we believed her. "We know that it's someplace her parents wouldn't want her to go. We can't see much of it in that champagne toasting snapshot. I'll try to ask around at the rehearsal tonight to find some possibilities. Speaking of the rehearsal, did I tell you that Barbara Wright insisted on doing a solo speech? I've been thinking of giving her Sonnet 29."

"Do you think she's emotionally ready to handle it?" Sophie asked.

"I guess we'll find out tonight."

Chapter 22

Barbara wasn't doing well with her sonnet.

When in disgrace with fortune and men's eyes,
I all alone beweep my outcast state,
And trouble deaf heaven with my bootless cries,
And look upon myself and curse my fate,
Wishing me like to one more rich in hope,
Featured like him, like him with friends possessed,
Desiring this man's art and that man's scope,
With what I most enjoy contented least,
Yet in these thoughts myself almost despising,
Haply I think on thee, and then my state,
(Like to the lark at break of day arising
From sullen earth) sings hymns at heaven's gate.
For thy sweet love remembered such wealth brings
That then I scorn to change my state with kings.

The other actors sat in embarrassed silence after Barbara completed reading the sonnet. They didn't know how to react. Should they applaud her performance as was customary procedure for the Little Players? Or should they show respect for her obvious emotional turmoil by remaining silent? So they sat there not knowing what to do or say. Would this be how they would from now on behave around Barbara, not knowing how to act so perhaps avoiding her altogether? It was up to me to help them out and teach them a little more about acting in the bargain.

I had distributed all the short scenes and monologues and had clarified the order they would be presented at the memorial. I had also asked RoseMarie Farrell, a soloist in the church choir, to sing two lovely songs also by Shakespeare. All the pieces were about love and friendship and loss, and the Little Players as well as Miss Laurence seemed to be pleased with my choices and thought the evening would turn out to be precisely what they had hoped it would be. After each selection was read, I gave a few relevant notes. The last piece was the moving love sonnet I had assigned to Barbara. She had broken down constantly while reading it saddening and, as I have said, embarrassing the others. It was time for me to speak up.

"All right, Barbara. We know how difficult this is for you to do, but if you still want to be part of this evening . . ."

"Oh, I do, Harry. I must be." She pulled another Kleenex from the box in front of her and dabbed again at her reddened eyes.

"If that's the case, Barbara, then you have to perform the piece well. I'm afraid all that you've recently had to endure has made you forget one of the main tenets of good acting. And that is something I've brought to the attention of all of you at one time or another.

"It is always essential for the actor to decide what his or her character is feeling every moment and then clearly and transparently express that emotion to the audience. The words the character speaks may seem sometimes to be in variance with those feelings, but it is the obligation of the actor to make clear to the audience what the character is truly feeling. A good case in point is your piece, Barbara.

"We have decided to treat the sonnets as little one-act plays and therefore you must decide who your character is, what emotions she is feeling, to whom she is speaking and why she is saying these words to the other character. This is what you as actors must do in every scene you play.

"Let's carefully study these fourteen lines to find answers to these questions. First of all who is the speaker? She is obviously someone in love with the man she is addressing and why is she saying these words to him? She is obviously telling him how much she loves him, how much her love for him means to her. She says she sometimes is depressed and worries even despairs about her life and how others see her, is jealous of others' success and so forth.

> When in disgrace with fortune and men's eyes . . .
>
> Wishing me like to one more rich in hope . . .
>
> Desiring this man's art and that man's scope . . .

When she is in that bad place, she says, then luckily she happens ("Haply") to remember how fortunate she really is to have this person in her life, and she realizes how foolish she was to be so blue, so depressed. She has much more than all the others she foolishly envied. She is the luckiest woman in the world.

> Haply I think on thee, and then my state . . .
>
> . . . sings hymns at heaven's gate.
>
> For thy sweet love remembered such wealth brings
>
> That then I scorn to change my state with kings.

"These last few lines express the reason she's speaking to her lover: she wants to tell him how much she loves him and how lucky she is to have him. And how stupid she is to be so melancholy sometimes when she has so much to be thankful for. So this little sonnet is actually a happy love message to the man she loves. It is a valentine.

"But because the first eight lines describe sad situations you—and many others I have heard read this sonnet—mistakenly played what the words seem to say and cried your eyes out. Instead, you should have fulfilled the actor's job of expressing what the character is actually feeling, not necessarily what the words seem to suggest. The speaker is expressing to her lover how happy she is to have him and so probably makes fun of herself as she relates how silly she is to be so melodramatically depressed sometimes when she has so much for which to be thankful.

"Barbara, I would like you to read the poem once more. And this time express how lucky and happy you are and how silly you sometimes are to feel otherwise."

She then stood up and correctly acted the piece. She laughed and made fun of herself when she exaggerated her feelings of despair in the first two quatrains. She made clear the love she was feeling all along in the final quatrain. She spoke the final rhyming couplet simply and full of genuine love and happiness. It was a revelation, a complete transformation. The other actors were stunned into silence once again. But this time in a good way. Then they broke out into ecstatic applause. Sophie and I joined them. One of the highlights of my life happened then: I looked at Barbara Wright and she was smiling.

Chapter

23

But I wasn't smiling when I was standing alone in front of Dr. Rodgers' residence. I had insisted that Sophie not accompany me on this visit. I told her I would meet her back at Madge's as soon as I had received the news. She was not happy about it but acceded to my wishes. Before I walked away from Laurence House, Sophie said to me, "You've done good work here tonight, boss. You've been a superhero to Barbara even without the tights. And as a superhero, you can lick anything in your path. Even kryptonite. Go get 'em, Superman: Up, up and away!"

The warm glow I felt from these words dissipated during the ten minute walk to the doctor's house. The chill in the night air seemed to have penetrated my insides, and my hand actually trembled a bit as I rang the doorbell. So much for being a superhero.

"Oh, it's you," the gruff voiced Basil grunted as he opened the door.

Does this pain in the you-know-what live here too? Just what I needed. That's what I was thinking but I merely said, "Good evening. Dr. Rodgers was kind enough to invite me over . . ."

"Yeah, she mentioned that," he interrupted as he let me inside. "She's on the phone now. You can sit in there if you like." Indicating with a jerk of his head a closed door to the right of the entry hall, he started to go up a flight of stairs.

"Uh, you will tell her I'm here, won't you?" I called out to his retreating back. Of course I received no answer. Feeling more than a bit of irritation, I followed his instruction and entered what turned out to be a small but very pleasant library. Although it was mid-June, there was a cozy fire crackling in the hearth. It felt good on this unusually cold night. The contents of the wall-lined bookshelves looked inviting. I noticed one section full of medical books, another with travel commentaries, another with good works of fiction, another . . . But then my attention was drawn to a familiar looking volume on the side table next to a small settee. I went over to it and picked it up. Yes, it was a copy of my best-seller *Five Days in May*. Was she a fan? I felt a little warmer. I removed my jacket, sat down and began flipping through the pages.

"Uh oh, you've discovered my little secret. I have been reading up on you, Mr. Hunt," Dr. Rodgers said with a laugh.

"I'm flattered, I think. And what have you learned?"

"For one thing that you have a history of headaches. The first line of your book tells me that." She turned to the page and read: "'As usual, I had a splitting headache.' I wonder if last night weren't the first time you received a head injury."

My mind flashed back to that fishing trip with my father. ("We are the merry Mouseketeers.") "I did hit my head once when I was seven. But since then headaches have always been associated with stress."

"And you have a lot of stress in your life. You certainly did during your time in Brookfield."

"Right, and there's even more now with the shooting of Tom Wright in the boat we were in and then the injury of our hostess' son. So, I've been having headaches."

"And there's no question that something hit the back of your head whether you remember it or not. And that has resulted in a pretty serious concussion. Although I'm happy to report that the scan reveals no evidence of interior bleeding, the results do show that you sustained a concussion."

I gulped. "What exactly is a concussion, doctor?"

"It's like a bruise that results from your brain colliding with your skull as a result of a head injury. About one million concussions occur in the US each year and there are likely many more people who have them and don't report them. Luckily, much research is being done about them and how to help your brain heal. The most common advice is to try to prevent additional brain injuries from occurring. So avoid activities that propose such a threat. This is of particular importance to student or professional athletes, NFL players for instance. The next good advice to recover fully is to institute total brain rest for a week, complete sensory deprivation. That means no computer, no music, no watching TV, as complete a rest as you can manage."

I gulped again. Total rest did not seem to be part of the job description of God's deputy or a member of the Justice League of America!

"Recent studies I've seen with soldiers who had suffered brain injuries concluded that they be fed as soon as possible. It is helpful for patients to get at least 50% of their usual caloric intake within 24 hours, including a higher-than-usual amount of protein, which should be continued for two weeks."

"I had a huge breakfast courtesy of Mrs. Donohue which included a lot of protein. And I was starved this afternoon and had fish. More protein tonight before the rehearsal."

"That's very good. And other research has shown that you should take a double dose of fish oil as quickly as possible after the injury and for up to a week afterward. This wouldn't be advised if we had seen evidence of bleeding in your brain."

"Wait, please, so I can write all this down. Oh, where's Sophie when you really need her?"

"Don't worry, Mr. Hunt. I have prepared some information sheets for you that describe all the natural ways you can help brain tissues heal."

She handed me a folder with my name on it. I gave a cursory glance inside and noticed such highlighted bullet points as: anti-oxidants in your diet, lots of fluids, amica pellets, Tylenol rather than Advil, etc. I knew that Sophie would ensure that I followed every one of these directives.

"During the next few days there is always the possibility—*albeit* a small one—that a blood clot could develop in your brain. Therefore, I would like you to visit me daily either at the medical center or here—whichever proves easier for you—for a brief neurological examination. Better safe than sorry, don't you agree?"

"I do, doctor. Thank you very much. I'm in your debt." That delicious smile again. What a pleasure it was to see that. "You certainly seem an expert in this line of medicine. Is that your specialty?"

"I have a particular interest in it, yes." I noticed that her smile faded as she said these words and she was silent for a moment. She looked at me and then seemed to make the decision to say, "Two years ago my son sustained brain injuries in a car crash."

"I hope he pulled through," I said without thinking. The sadness I then saw in her eyes told me he hadn't. I felt like cutting out my tongue.

"No, he didn't," she almost whispered.

To change the subject as quickly as I could, I asked if the man who was with her each time I've seen her was also a specialist on brain injuries.

She looked at me in amazement. "You mean, Basil? Oh, no. He's my brother-in-law and a dentist, the only dentist in town." She then laughed a bit and added, "If you were suffering from a tooth ache, you would be seeing him right now rather than me."

In a flash, the line from *As You Like It* detailing the seventh and final age of man "sans TEETH, sans eyes, sans taste, sans everything" popped into my mind for the third time. And suddenly I knew why it had been bouncing around in my subconscious. It was because in the final stage of Tom Wright's life he had uttered these last words to me:

"Aches . . . Tooth . . . Aches . . . Tooth . . . Tooths . . . Aches . . . ."

Chapter 24

"YOU SUDDENLY LOOK PRETTY STRANGE, Mr. Hunt."

"Uh, yeah. Thinking of dentists always seems to agitate me, doctor."

"Well, as you know, agitation is exactly what you don't want. You need to rest your body and your mind. How about a cup of herbal tea?"

"That would be wonderful, thank you."

As she opened the door to leave the library, she looked down and smiled. "And this is the third and final member of my little domicile. Mr. Hunt, please say hello to Roscoe."

The handsome white dog looked up at me. He had apparently been sitting patiently outside the closed door. "Hello, Roscoe. I'm pleased to meet you." I held my hand out to him with the palm open, and without hesitation he came over to me and licked it.

"Roscoe is the sweetest, friendliest dog in the world," she said lovingly. He's just about perfect. I sometimes think of him as St. Roscoe."

"He's a beauty all right," I concurred patting him. I could see now that although predominantly white, Roscoe had one black spot over each eye and another on his hind quarters that only added to his overall appeal. He was a charmer. That's for sure. And he seemed to like me.

"You've made quite an impression with Roscoe . . . and with me, Mr. Hunt." There was that smile again that melted my heart.

"If the professional part of our visit is over, would you call me, Harry? Please?"

"Why not, Harry. I'm Ruth Catherine." And with that she left to make the tea. Roscoe rolled over on his side so I could rub his tummy. I was happy to oblige. I thought of Lucy, who had once belonged to my friend Charlie. She had loved to have her stomach rubbed as well. And I questioned what Ruth Catherine (How easily her name rolled in my thoughts) had just said: the dog, the unpleasant brother-in-law dentist and she comprised her entire household? Did that mean there was no husband around?

The tea was pleasant. The conversation was even more so. As we sat side by side on the settee in front of the comforting hearth with Roscoe lying on a rug at our feet, we talked about many things. To begin with, our family background: I was an only child. She had three sisters. Since her mother's favorite biblical story was the Book of Ruth, she gave that name to each of her daughters. They were differentiated with a distinctive middle name. The lovely lady sitting beside me was Ruth Catherine. Her elder sister was named Ruth Madeline; the younger was Ruth Eileen. She asked me about the childhood incident in the boat that resulted in my first head injury. The incident that led to my aversion to boats. She told me she wasn't sure if there were an officially named phobia for that but defined thalassophobia as the fear of the sea, hydrophobia as the fear of water, and thanatophobia as the fear of dying. I told her (a bit) about my relationship with my father (strained), with Sophie (devoted if complicated) and with Belinda (definitely complicated). And then she told me about her husband, her late husband. Sadly he had died in the same car crash as had their son. Although he had been flawed (as she put it), she had loved him. Their deaths had prompted her to pick up from their home in suburban Maryland and move in with the merry dentist, her late husband's brother, in his two-family house in Havenport. She decided to open a much needed medical center nearby a year ago. She was beginning to feel more comfortable in her new surroundings, though it had taken some time.

Roscoe had fallen asleep and was snoring a bit. It only ratcheted up his cute factor. Both Ruth Catherine and I were also rather tired, so we said good night. At the front door she told me not to forget to drop by tomorrow. I told her I didn't need the reminder. We both smiled.

When I got back to the Magill home, Sophie was a wreck. I apologized profusely about not calling her immediately with the good news that there had been no internal bleeding. That calmed her down considerably. I told her that there had been a concussion though. I handed her the information sheets for her perusal and mentioned that "Ruth Catherine" wanted me to check in with her for the next few days. Sophie picked up on the name at once.

"So you're on a first name basis now?" I dismissed the implication with a snort, but I think I did blush a little. "And what's with her using two first names? That's a little odd, isn't it?"

"I understand it's a family tradition, or some such thing. Anyway, it's imperative that I get a lot of rest, and our jabbering on and on is not helpful. Good night, Sophie." She seemed surprised when I stormed off to bed like that. I was a bit surprised as well.

Unfortunately, I wasn't able to fall right asleep. Try as I might to relax my injured brain, I couldn't prevent my thoughts from galloping apace. Had there really been someone behind me on the beach who had hit me from behind? If so who was he? What exactly had Tom tried to communicate to me with his dying breath? Was he alluding to the only dentist in town? Was brother-in-law Basil the laughing sniper? Or was I being ridiculous? I made a mental note to go over this in detail with Sophie in the morning. And thinking of her brother-in-law brought my thoughts of course back to Ruth Catherine and her nurturing nature and sensuous smile . . .

. . . and then I felt my father shaking me and severely repeating over and over, "Harrison. Harrison. Listen to me. Stop crying. Be a man. Don't be a baby. Be a man. "Your name is Harrison Hunt. It is the name of a man. Not a baby." No, he was wrong. My father was wrong. Harrison Hunt was not only the name of a man but the secret identify of a superman. The inner song in my head changed from the Mouseketeer tune to the theme song of my other favorite television show. I saw myself as George Reeves taking off his glasses and ripping open his shirt to reveal the giant "S." Alone in the boat hearing the splintering sound and feeling the cold water drenching my sneakers and socks, I looked at the shrinking form of my father swimming manically through the rising waves pursuing the elusive oars and I knew I would be safe. In fact I would save both of us. I would save the entire world for I was:

> Faster than a speeding bullet.
>
> More powerful than a locomotive.
>
> Able to leap tall buildings in a single bound.

And when the boat collided with the outcroppings of rocks, there was nothing to fear. All I had to do was simply fly out of the sinking boat and land gracefully on top of the rocks.

Up, up and away!

So what if I injured my head badly in the process? So what if I lost consciousness? What did it matter? All that I did, I did proudly and heroically

For truth, justice and the American way!

I woke up. As usual, I had a splitting headache.

Chapter 25

It was after 10:00 AM Monday morning when I finally came downstairs and met Sophie in the kitchen. She had already been "downtown" to purchase all the naturopathic items on the doctor's lists and had compiled and printed out an appropriate hour-by-hour regimen for me to follow. Mrs. Donohue had prepared a protein-rich breakfast for me that I gobbled up with gusto. Sophie brushed aside my attempt to apologize for snapping at her last night with a nonchalant wave of her hand, a smile and a bit of advice.

"Today, I suggest that you get all the rest you can, boss."

"But, Sophie," I protested, "We have so many critical investigative tasks still to accomplish."

"The operative word is WE. I'll do the field work and bring whatever I unearth to you for analysis, while you do the even more important work of assisting your brain tissues to heal. You won't be of any help to the people we care about if your condition gets worse. Think about it, Harry. Am I right, or am I right?"

I flashed her a conciliatory grin. "I'm sorry, Sophie, I choose not to think at this moment. I'm giving my 'cute little grey cells' a rest."

She showed me her to-do list for the day. I amended one or two details and then removed myself to lie down on the comfortable, pillow-strewn sofa in the sun room. Through the glass walls, I could see that it was less overcast outside than it had been for most of the weekend. A good omen I thought as I closed my eyes.

When I awoke it magically was lunchtime. While ingesting more protein accompanied by fish-oil pills and amica pellets, Sophie told me her news.

"At the rehearsal last night, as casually as I could I asked several of the actors to suggest some places both upscale and a little naughty not too far away that would be fun to go to. Remember, Edward told Roxanne that he and Sally were sneaking off to somewhere her parents wouldn't approve. I got some weird looks from many of the Little Players. Robby Donohue gave me the weirdest one when he overheard me but didn't say anything. Anyway, I did obtain the names of four spots. They told me they hadn't been there themselves but heard they were both expensive and a bit dicey. All of them, however, are located in the state capital a good hour away. One is a strip joint, one a disco-like dance hall and the other two are small, alternative music clubs. I looked at their web sites this morning. None seemed to resemble the photo on Edward's phone. But I think they should all be visited in person just to make sure."

"Didn't we pass some sort of a jazz club coming back from the airport right next door to the king-size version of Cousin Carrie's? That's closer to Havenport than the others."

"Right, The Copper Moon, the one that advertised "Hot Jazz, Cold Drinks.' I thought of it right away. When I asked about it, I was told it was very nice and very respectable. Some of them had been there several times and highly recommended it."

"That unfortunately doesn't sound like a place that requires a cover story to go to," I observed. "Still we should add it to our list to investigate. Don't forget to ask Noah Benson for his thoughts on this subject. A livery owner should know all the local dives. I was very disappointed that he and his wife missed the rehearsal last night."

"Me too. Miss Laurence told us they promised to be there tonight. The business trip they were on would be over today. I have plenty of questions for the dear little Bensons. Harry, I also got a call from—Do I dare mention his name?—Officer Krupke of the state police. He wanted to know more about the two cleaning women we saw at the airport. The personnel records revealed that all the airport cleaners are men and all of them were accounted for. I gave him their descriptions once again as best I could but could provide no further information about them. I also used this opportunity to ask him if Edward's fingerprints had been found at Cousin Carrie's at the airport. He very politely said he was sorry but that was confidential police information that couldn't be revealed to laymen. Laymen, indeed. 'Dear Officer Krupke,'" she sang hilariously off-key, "'Krup you!'"

I would have laughed longer had Sophie not given me a sharp glance while she pointed directly at my skull. "Sorry, boss. The last thing I want to do is over-excite you. But old habits die hard." She saw that I was about to comment on her remark but beat me to it by saying, "Now that must be a line from Shakespeare." I shook my head. "No, then it must be from a 16th century Scottish proverb, yes?"

"I'm afraid not, Sophie. It's actually credited to one Jeremy Belknap, an 18th century American clergyman from New Hampshire who wrote the first modern history written by an American. *The History of New*

Hampshire is quite a fascinating study, very thorough in its research, annotation and reporting. You should read it sometime."

"When will I learn to keep my big fat mouth shut?" Sophie groaned.

CHAPTER 26

WHEN I THEN ADMITTED TO Sophie my completely unsubstantiated suspicion that Tom Wright's murderer could possibly be the disagreeable dentist because of his profession, I'm afraid it did seem pretty farfetched. And Sophie thought so too. "I concede that some of the words Tom tried to say to you did sound like 'tooth aches,' but we'll need a lot more proof than that before we'll be sure we've found our man. I agree with you that he is rude and unpleasant. But lack of social skills does not necessarily a murderer make."

"Of course you're right, Sophie. But just to ease my mind, I'd like to do a little checking on him. Perhaps I can find out something when I visit Dr. Rodgers' house tonight after the rehearsal."

"Oh, you mean Ruth Catherine?" The exaggerated, lovey-dovey way Sophie intoned the name would have infuriated me once again had she not heartily laughed the moment after she had made her little (and I do mean little) joke. But I deigned to ignore it. After all I was starting to feel fatigued once again, and both Sophie and I felt it would be a good idea for me to take another nap before we went back to Laurence House for the next rehearsal.

Instead of counting sheep to lull me to sleep, I amused myself by counting dentists, that is, dentists as depicted in the movies. The first one that came to mind was of course the Nazi dentist Dr. Christian Szell in *Marathon Man* played so menacingly by Laurence Olivier. I cringed to remember what poor Dustin Hoffman had to go through in that chair. I next quickly thought of another horror movie dentist, Steve Martin's comically sadistic biker who enlivened the musical version of *Little Shop of Horrors*. I became drowsier as I pictured the animated dentist with the spoiled daughter in *Finding Nemo*. As I came up with Campbell Scott as the dentist whose wife might be having an affair in the aptly titled *The Secret Life of Dentists*, I dropped off.

I awoke later than I had planned. Dinner and preparing for today's rehearsal took longer than expected, so we were a little late arriving at Laurence House. Miss Laurence was waiting in the grand but slightly faded vestibule as we walked in. She seemed relieved to see us. "Oh, my dear Mr. Hunt and Miss Xerxes, I'm so delighted you're here. I was so worried you would not be able to continue sharing your expertise at our little rehearsals."

"Worried?" I asked.

"Why yes, of course. When I heard from so many friends in the village the nature of your distressing disorder, I was both consumed with concern and plagued with guilt for forcing you to tax the last remaining residue of your strength to help us in our hour of need. Oh, Mr. Hunt, will you ever be able to forgive my insensitivity and selfishness?"

For a moment I was at a loss to know where to begin to respond to her torrent of emotion. "Thank you for your concern, Miss Laurence, but I'm not at death's door yet," I replied with a smile.

"Marry, heaven forbid!" she exclaimed clutching at her heart.

Sophie looked questioningly at me. I silently mouthed, *Othello*, then proceeded. "No, actually Miss Laurence, I've had a small concussion that's all. Nothing to worry about."

"Then your two visits to Dr. Rodgers in the same day—one even in the dead of night—and the purchase by Miss Xerxes of medicinal remedies at break of day . . ."

"Were merely preventative," I said quickly before mouthing "double Shakespeare!" to Sophie.

Miss Laurence sighed a breath of relief and as she led us into the sitting room quoted for the second time, "I can no other answer make, but, thanks, and thanks, and thanks" I turned to Sophie and raised my eyebrows. She paused for a moment then triumphantly answered, *Twelfth Night*. I gave her two thumbs up, and we joined the Little Players.

They had all shown relief when told they needn't worry further about my health. "Even Robby had seemed a little worried," Sophie said with an edge. "I can hardly believe it."

"Aw, come on, Sophie. He is only doing his duty," I said magnanimously. I knew she wanted to reply with her famous "Bull crap" expletive, but she had the good sense to hold her tongue.

* * *

> Under the greenwood tree
>
> Who loves to lie with me,
>
> And turn his merry note
>
> Unto the sweet bird's throat,
>
> Come hither, come hither, come hither!
>
> Here shall he see

No enemy

But winter and rough weather.

With the final chords, the song ended. We were all so moved that we sat still for a moment before bursting into applause. RoseMarie Farrell accompanied by Miss Laurence on the piano had sung the love song from *As You Like It* simply, charmingly, beautifully. It would be a lovely ending to the first part of the memorial.

"Good work, everyone. Let's take a ten-minute break," I said with a smile.

As her fellow actors complimented the obviously delighted singer, Sophie said to me, "Look how touched Barbara is by the song and I think by everyone's performance."

I turned to look at Barbara sitting a little by herself at one side of the room. There were tears in her eyes. But I think they were tears of gratitude rather than grief. The half-crazed woman I had seen at the church was gone. "She knows by the way they express their feelings for Tom through the passages they're reading just how much they all truly cared for him. It's made a world of difference in her. She certainly was right in deciding to be a part of the show." The other performers walked over to Barbara and they were now all comfortably talking.

"They certainly must be working hard on their own. There's been a big improvement since last evening."

"I agree, Sophie. And they'll continue to improve. They're more motivated to do a great job on this than I've ever seen them. However, I'm more than disappointed that the Bensons haven't shown up yet, even though they called Miss Laurence again this morning and assured her they'd be here tonight. I wish I knew where they were. Damn, we've got to find out who killed Tom and what happened to Sally. Not only for Barbara but now for the whole village's sake."

"We'll do just that, boss. I'm sure of it. We just need one good break, that's all."

Amazingly enough, these words were no sooner out of her mouth than Sophie's cell phone rang. I was prevented from listening to her conversation by Robby Donohue. He asked me to clarify the scansion of two of his lines from Orlando's comic declaration of his love for Rosalind. A number of the pieces in the show were from *As You Like It,* the Bard's depiction of love in all its many guises.

Sophie interrupted us. "Excuse me, boss. But I've got great news. That was Madge calling me from the hospital. Edward has improved. His condition is now listed as still very serious but stable. Who says there are no such things as miracles?"

Before either Robby or I could comment, his cell phone loudly rang as well. "What the . . ." he said as he answered the call. I assumed he was also being informed of the change in Edward's condition. But the startled look on his face made me think otherwise. He turned his back to us as he answered the call. The ringing of the two phones had gotten everyone's attention, and all the Little Players silently watched Robby's back as he spoke in lowered tones. In a minute or two he hung up and turned to face us. His face was white as snow. In a choked voice he said, "There's been an accident out at sea: an explosion on board Noah and Nora Benson's boat The Sea Witch. They've both been killed."

Chapter 27

"Be careful what you wish for." This was the first of two thoughts I couldn't get out of my head. Sophie had wished for one good break in the case. She immediately received the promising news that Edward's condition had improved. Perhaps he would be conscious soon and we would learn from him what had really happened. But then I had wished we also find out why the Bensons hadn't shown up for rehearsals. That wish was also immediately granted with Robby's shocking announcement. This prompted my second thought: "If wishes were horses." No more wishes from now on, I vowed, only action.

And there was suddenly plenty of action. Robby had rushed out of the building, obviously summoned to the scene of the tragedy. Barbara Wright let out a scream and started mumbling such rhetorical questions as: "How many more deaths will there be?" and "When will this end?" and "When will Justice be served?" Of course she gazed directly at me as she intoned that one. Barbara was not the only one expressing dismay. All the Little Players were talking at once; some openly wept.

Good old Sophie then stepped up to the plate. "I think we should end the rehearsal now. We all need to take time to assess this terrible news. I know Miss Laurence has once again prepared some warm beverages in the East Room. A good hot cup of tea might do us all some good."

"Or something a damn-sight stronger!" was the apt suggestion of Ray Gross the elderly farmer.

Dabbing at her eyes with a lavender colored hankie, Miss Laurence led the others into the next room. Sophie slowly sat down next to me. "Well, that's a kick in the pants."

"What a horrible thing to happen." It was simpler for me to state the obvious than to attempt to comprehend and deal with this new crisis.

But not Sophie. She had already turned on the laptop she always carried to rehearsals to record the notes I gave the actors, script alterations, and the like. She had pulled up the website for the Bensons' limousine and charter boat service. She clicked on a link and read out loud:

Welcome Aboard the Sea Witch!!!

> Thank you for choosing Benson Charters for your next sea fishing trip. We are proud to offer some of the state's best deep sea fishing charters including Shark Fishing and Giant Bluefin Tuna Fishing. Inshore saltwater fishing for Striped Bass, Stripers, Bluefish and Mackerel. Ground saltwater fishing for Cod and Haddock. We also offer ocean cruises and tours from Havenport including Seal and Whale Watching, Dinner and Sunset Cruises, and Scenic Island Tours.

The Sea Witch is a 22 foot BlueCoastal center console, powered by a Honda four stroke outboard motor. BlueCoastal power boats are incredibly safe, dry and stable. The BlueCoastal Hull has plenty of fishing space along with comfortable bench seating and a flat "non-skid" deck. The Honda 225 horsepower outboard is fast, unbelievably quiet, and has a clean smoke free exhaust that is friendly to anglers as well as the environment.

The combination of a BlueCoastal Hull, a Honda outboard motor, Furono G.P.S., and all the requisite safety equipment make this vessel the perfect fishing machine!

Your affable hosts are Nora and Noah Benson. Your seasoned captain is Billy Lee Baxter.

Welcome Aboard the Sea Witch for an adventure you'll remember for the rest of your life!

The irony of the last line was not lost on us. After Sophie closed the laptop, I said, "I hope for God's sake that the captain was not also on board. Robby only mentioned the Bensons. I believe Tom Wright introduced me to Billy Lee Baxter once or twice. Have you met him, Sophie?

"I don't think so. I also hope he's safe and sound. And if he is, he should be the next person we contact." I looked at her quizzically. "Boss, there's been one murder already, possibly two. We suspect there might be something fishy about the Bensons' tie-in with Edward. Who's to say they weren't victims of foul play as well?"

"Who indeed?"

We spent some time bonding with the Little Players before they sorrowfully left for the night. They now seemed even more determined to put on a stellar memorial on Thursday and were looking forward to fine tuning the performance at the final two evening rehearsals. Sophie and I stayed and talked with Barbara after the others had gone. She seemed calmer now and perked up when I decided to tell her that I had a theory that Sally and Edward went to a night spot that Barbara or Tom wouldn't have chosen for her. I asked her if she could help us identify the venue. She said she remembered hearing about some place with a shady reputation. She said she'd get back to us on this. Her demeanor seemed more assured when she left us. Giving her something to do to assist us seemed a very good idea.

Sophie told me she had a lot of things to check this evening and hoped my treatment with Dr. Rodgers would be helpful. I knew she was trying to please me when she used that title in referring to Ruth Catherine.

So once again I soon was standing outside the doctor's home and once again the wind was blowing. The temperature had dropped once again this evening, but I don't think that was the only reason why I shook a little as I rang the doorbell.

I was surprised that Ruth Catherine seemed a little on edge and distracted as she asked me to lie down on the settee and make myself comfortable. "As I've told you, Harry, much further research still needs to be done on the effects of concussion on the brain and on cognitive function. However, there has been treatment available in the form of specific types of neurotherapy such as EEG Biofeedback. This is what I'd like to start you on tonight. With biofeedback, you're connected to electrical sensors that help you receive information about your body functions. This feedback helps you focus on making subtle changes in your body, such as relaxing certain muscles to achieve the results you want, such as reducing pain. The headaches are still there, right? In essence, biofeedback in a way may give you the power to use your thoughts to control you own body. It's often used as a relaxation technique as well."

As she said this, she dropped the sensors she was about to attach to my head. "I'm sorry I'm so clumsy tonight. I probably could benefit using that technique myself right now." She laughed as she made that comment, but she definitely did seem to be under some stress.

"Are you all right? Is something the matter?"

"No, not really. I'm afraid I just have something on my mind." She laughed again at the unintended pun she made while at the same time manipulating the little electronic gizmos to my skull.

"Is it about the Sea Witch?" I asked.

I was surprised by her reaction. "What, how do you know about that?"

I told her how and, in turn, she said that her brother-in-law had just called her from the medical center about the disaster a few minutes before I came by. A patient of his had given him the information. "The news upset me," she continued. "I've known the Bensons since I moved here. It was quite a shock."

"I know. It was to me as well. I tell you what. How about our postponing this procedure until tomorrow evening? I think by then I should be in a mood more conducive to mastering a relaxation technique."

She smiled. "All right. I'll take you up on that. I hope we'll both be in a better state by then."

I smiled back and started to get up. I noticed that the delightful dog Roscoe who had been lying peacefully on his dog mat near the fireplace suddenly started pacing nervously around the room and panting. "Is something wrong with Roscoe?"

"Oh, the poor thing. He's always so calm and well-behaved except when he hears certain loud noises, like thunder. He becomes terrified when he hears them."

"Is it thundering? I don't hear anything," I said.

"But Roscoe does. He must be sensing the rumblings of a thunderstorm a distance from us. See, he tries to hide in the smallest space he can find when that happens."

The dog did seem to be in a panic, attempting to position himself in each corner of the room and under the furniture. Ruth Catherine then opened the library door and Roscoe shot out of the room. "He'll go into the bathroom now and get himself wedged somehow into the tiny space between the sink and the toilet. He feels more secure there."

We both jumped as a tremendous clap of thunder rattled the house. "You see, Roscoe knows. If you don't mind, I'll go in there with him now and try to get him to relax a bit."

"Why don't you try biofeedback with him?" I said with a chuckle.

She laughed once again. "Maybe I will at that. Please take an umbrella from the stand near the front door." She started to walk in the direction Roscoe had taken.

"Thank you. I'll return it tomorrow night," I called after her. I took an umbrella and started to open the front door when a sound startled me. Ruth Catherine's brother-in-law was descending the stairs from the second floor. He nodded curtly to me then proceeded into the next room. He had been upstairs all the time. Why had she told me he had just called her from the medical center twenty miles away?

CHAPTER 28

THERE WERE MORE CLAPS OF thunder and some flashes of lightning as I walked the short distance to the Magill house. But I barely noticed them. My mind was racing. Did Ruth Catherine lie to me? Why would she do that? Was there another simple explanation for the discrepancy? If so, what could it be? When I became aware that my headache had worsened, I tried to curtail this fruitless brainstorming. This was not the best activity for me to pursue at this time, medically or emotionally. As I opened the front door, the heavens opened up as well.

"Well, you just missed the downpour. You're a lucky fella," Sophie said to me.

"Yeah, very lucky." I begged off further discussion by telling Sophie I felt really tired and needed to go to bed. I took the holistic remedies she had laid out for me then climbed the stairs. I wondered why I hadn't told Sophie about the inconsistency in the doctor's explanation. Oh well, it was probably nothing.

When I came downstairs for breakfast Tuesday morning, I found Sophie and Mrs. Donohue in the den watching television. "I hoped it didn't wake you, Mr. Hunt. I kept the volume down as low as I could. I'll go put your breakfast on the table now."

"No, that's all right, Mrs. Donohue. You stay here and watch the news. I'll serve breakfast," Sophie said as she and I moved to the kitchen.

I asked Sophie what was going on. She told me that Mrs. Donohue had heard a news flash on the radio a short time ago. They had then turned on the TV.

"About the boat explosion?" I surmised.

Sophie nodded. "It's all over the airwaves. The police have just informed the media. I guess we are the only ones who got word of it last night." I didn't say anything while she transferred the protein-rich victuals Mrs. Donohue had prepared to the table.

Then she continued, "I've taken down the pertinent details. The Bensons were apparently alone on the boat when it blew up. The police preliminary report conjectured that escaping gas fumes may have been ignited by something, possibly equipment that was already running on the boat. The bodies were terribly burned, and it would seem that they died instantly in the explosion. The bodies were taken to the hospital by the coast guard. The same way Tom Wright's body was. After the fires were extinguished, the Sea Witch was towed to the police lab a few miles from the hospital. That took a number of hours longer than expected because of the rough seas caused by the storm last night." She then looked up from her notebook and asked, "Were you able to sleep well last night or did the noise of the thunderstorm keep you up, as it did me?"

"No, I slept pretty soundly actually."

"Well, there must be something to that neurotherapy of Dr. Rodgers after all."

"Yes," I looked away. "There must be. I'll be going back there tonight to continue it." I hated telling half-truths to Sophie. But for some reason I felt compelled to do that.

"Okay. Now, I have drawn up a to-do list for me today that I'd like you to look at."

Before she could continue, her cell phone rang. I had eaten a substantial portion of my breakfast when she hung up.

"That was Billy Lee Baxter, the captain of the Sea Witch returning my call. He sounded really broken up, but agreed to see me. He lives not far from the wharf. I'll let you know what I find out."

"Sophie, I'd like to go with you. I know I'm supposed to rest, but I'm feeling quite a bit better and I'm getting a little stir crazy staying alone in the house all day. What do you say?"

"I guess so, boss. But please don't exert yourself. I want you to get better."

"So do I, Sophie. And now that I'm Mr. Biofeedback, I know how to make myself relax. So there's nothing to worry about." Once again, I felt more than a twinge of guilt misleading Sophie. But it got her to agree, and I wanted very much to question the captain live and in person.

While I finished my morning meal, Sophie related her Tuesday To-Do List. After our forthcoming meeting on the wharf, she wanted to drive up to the main branch of Cousin Carrie's Home Cooking to get as much additional information from the formidable Jessie Gillespie as she could.

"And if you remain calm and relaxed during our first interview, who knows, maybe I'll grant you the great honor of accompanying me there as well."

"A dream come true," I smirked.

We looked in on Mrs. Donohue to tell her we were going out. She was still glued to the television set. "Anything new?" I asked. "No, but they keep showing pictures of the Bensons' boat. Just terrible!" We saw what she meant. The Sea Witch was now just a burned-out shell. "I was finally able to reach Robby," she added. He spent all night helping out the state police. He sounds exhausted. First Tom gets shot, then Sally goes missing, then Edward tries to kill himself, and now poor, poor Nora and Noah. How could all this happen in Havenport?"

It was a question we couldn't answer. Yet.

We spotted Billy Lee Baxter at the wharf not far from his house. He was in my mind the quintessential 'old salt.' He was in his sixties or seventies, thin as a rail with skin toughened like leather from exposure to sun and wind. His captain's hat was pulled low over his sharp features. He was inspecting the remaining charter boat owned by Noah Benson, the Norah B, whose name brought tears to Sophie's eyes. Mine too maybe. This boat was much smaller than the Sea Witch. "There are a few minor damages caused by the storm," he told us. "They can easily be repaired. But the other one, she's gone, gone for good. She was a beauty. And I loved her. Almost as much as I loved Nora and Noah. And they're now all gone, gone for good. And for what? Some stupid, freakin' fluke."

"What do you mean, Billy Lee?"

"Well, Mr. Hunt, it had to be some crazy accident. Noah was a good sailor. He knew all about safety precautions. But weird things can happen. While Diesel fuel has a flash point around 140 degrees, gasoline can burn at 40 below zero! A cuppa gas can equal more than a stick of dynamite when ignited. Good boat manufacturers like BlueCoastal do their best to keep sparks and gasoline away from each other. But the rest is up to us."

'When was the boat's last check-up?" Sophie asked.

"I did one last week before I took a fishing party out. Everything was ship-shape. I look the ship over every time she's going out. If I had known Noah was going to take her out again on Sunday, I would have done another routine check. But he called me at the last minute and told me he and Nora were going to meet with an important customer on his yacht and didn't need me to come along. They did this every few months or so, but nothin' terrible like this ever happened."

"Did he tell you who the customer was?" I asked.

"No he didn't, Mr. Hunt. But since he stayed out for two days, it might have required refuelin' and that's the time that most freak accidents occur. All good boaters like Noah know to turn off all power before and during fuelin'. Electricity is less likely to spark if it's not flowin'. Then, after fuelin', it's always wise to inspect the bilge area and, of course, turn on exhaust blowers before startin' the engine for at least four or five minutes. Another common mistake is not operatin' the exhaust blowers while at anchor or beached with a generator runnin'. But I'm sure Noah would have followed these procedures as a matter of course. But sometimes freak accidents happen. Sometimes somethin' can clog the exhaust blowers so they're not effective. Somethin' like that could possibly have taken place. It's the only thing I can think of. There was an incident down East I heard about last fall. When a gasoline-powered boat exploded after re-fuelin' even after the boaters had run the blowers for the recommended time, it turned out that they were ineffective because a bird's nest was blockin' the vent system. A freakin' bird's nest! If I only had the chance to go over the boat before they set off, maybe I could have found the problem. Maybe I could have saved the lives of Nora and Noah. Maybe I could have saved my beautiful boat. Oh God, I wish. I wish to God I could have prevented this. I wish to God!"

If wishes were horses, I thought as we left the old salt staring out to sea sobbing.

We drove along in silence while my thoughts grew blacker and blacker. Suddenly I exploded: "A bird's nest! A bird's nest clogging an air vent once caused tremendous devastation and could very well have caused last night's horror for all we know! What did he call all this . . . a freaking fluke? Could all our lives be hanging on a fluke, a chance bit of fate, a toss of the dice by the universe? Maybe Gloucester is dead-on when he says in *Lear*:

> As flies to wanton boys are we to the gods.
> They kill us for their sport."

Sophie wisely waited for my outburst to abate before she calmly said: "Harry, you know you don't really mean that. Though some things may be the result of chance or luck (good or bad), not everything is. Maybe the Bensons died as a result of a freak accident. But maybe they didn't. Let's do our best to find out which it was. We know for sure that it weren't the gods who for sport murdered Charlie and Robert in Brookfield. Only through hard work and conscious effort did we find out who really did it. And it will be by hard work and conscious effort that we'll find out who killed Tom Wright. Was it Edward or someone else? Maybe we'll be a little closer to discovering the truth when we talk again to Mrs. Gillespie. Let's do that now, okay?"

"Okay, Sophie. I'll get down from my soapbox now."

"A dream come true," Sophie said with a twinkle in her eye.

Manderville led us directly to the main branch of Cousin Carrie's in record time. We looked once again at the supersized version of the Cape Cod themed cottage we had visited twice before. This was the first time however that we had seen it in broad daylight I am loath to admit that the painted sea gulls and lighthouse which decorated the exterior did appear marginally less tacky this time.

The now familiar restaurant review laminated and enlarged in poster format greeted us once again at the reservation desk. It looked a little different to me, but I was distracted by another greeting: this time by a smiling hostess who asked, "Table for two?"

"Maybe a little later, but first we'd like to have a word with the regional manager, Mrs. Jessie Gillespie," Sophie said in her most professional manner. "Is she around?"

"She is," the hostess replied but then lowered her voice as she added, "Listen, you might be better off seeing Mrs. Gillespie another time. Especially if you're trying to sell her something. She's in one of her rampages now, and you might want to get out while the getting is good."

"Thanks for your warning, but we'd still like to see her."

"Don't say I didn't warn you. Mari," the hostess called to a young waitress, "Would you mind finding Mrs. Gillespie and telling her she has visitors. She may be in the back. Your names please?"

I started to say "Harri . . ." but Sophie stopped me. "We'd prefer to make this a surprise, if you don't mind."

With a shrug, the waitress went off on her mission, and the hostess told us we could wait in the little bar area to the left of the entrance. As she pointed in that direction, I noticed something that surprised me. "Sophie," I whispered. "Look at her left hand."

"What do you mean, Harry?" she whispered back. Then she saw it too. Her eyes widened with recognition. It was a small purplish-red spot in the shape of a half circle. It was an exact duplicate to the birthmark we had noticed on the back of Edward's left hand.

Chapter 29

I HAD NO IDEA WHAT to say or do next. I couldn't just ask a perfect stranger to let me examine her birthmark or whatever it was, could I? I looked at Sophie with a bewildered air. The way she looked back at me betrayed her confusion as to how to proceed. However, we were spared further unease by the hostess herself.

Lelia (for that was the name identified on her nametag) couldn't miss the way we were gawking at her hand. "Oh, geez," she seemed mildly embarrassed. "That darn thing is so hard to wash off, and it takes just forever to wear away by itself."

"I beg your pardon?" I replied with what I hoped was a nonchalant manner.

"That darn stamp they press on your hand to show you've paid your cover charge."

"They?" Sophie's voice echoed my casual tone.

"The folks next door at The Copper Moon. A friend and I went there last night after work. I had thought I had washed that darn thing off. I guess they make it so hard to get rid of as a way to get some free advertising. Not that they need it."

"The Copper Moon is a popular place?" I hoped I appeared to be merely making small talk.

"You bet. There's always a line waiting to get in. The entertainment is always great and the food and drinks are first rate. It would usually be out of my pay scale, but the guy who took me there last night didn't seem to mind. Am I a lucky gal, or what?"

"I'm sure he's the lucky one," Sophie diplomatically said.

"Gee thanks," Lelia giggled. "I sorta think so too."

Before we all became BFFs (another expression I believe I had picked up from poor Sally like 'bummer'), the waitress returned. "Mrs. Gillespie is busy in a meeting right now, and she doesn't care to be interrupted, if you know what I mean," she rolled her eyes to the hostess who nodded her head sympathetically. Apparently Mrs. Gillespie was as loved by her employees as she was by us.

"Thanks anyway," I said. "We'll try to catch her another time." Since it was lunchtime, I added, "While we're here, we might as well have a bite." The hostess advised Mari to seat us at table 37, next to a pretty enough little vignette of faux seagulls sitting atop a number of picturesque lobster pots and fishing nets. We ordered (Dr. Rodgers would be pleased with my fish selections.) then decided to look around a bit before our food arrived. Perhaps we would just happen to run into Mrs. Gillespie and get some pertinent questions answered.

"I feel like kicking myself," Sophie said as we casually walked through a side door marked Employees Only. "The shape and color of the mark on Edward's hand matched the big sign outside the night club, and I never made the connection. And for the life of me, it never crossed my hand that the mark was a somewhat faded rubber stamp marking. Some detective I am!"

"Make that two. I feel like quite a fool myself. Anyway, it does seem likely now that we've discovered where Sally and Edward were Saturday night. But from what we've heard of the place, it doesn't sound in any way disreputable. Let's get in there sometime to verify if the interior matches the photo on his phone."

"Sounds like a plan," said Sophie. There were a number of closed doors which branched off the corridor down which we were walking. The first one was marked Office. Sophie knocked quietly. No one replied. As she opened the door to the darkened room she whispered, "If anyone catches us, we'll just tell them we're looking for the restrooms."

"Sounds like a plan," I mimicked her. She switched on the office lights and stuck her tongue out at me simultaneously. If there's one strong suit of Sophie's, it is her ability to multitask.

I wasn't quite sure what we were looking for, if anything, but Sophie dutifully recorded the major contents of the room in her ever-handy notebook. A small printing press in the corner of the room attracted my attention. I saw that the daily specials to the menu were printed here and also . . .

"Sophie, come look at this," I whispered. I pointed out to her three piles of posters printed on heavy stock. Two of the piles had already been laminated; the remaining posters were lying next to the compact machine reserved for this function, perhaps to be completed when the operator returned from lunch. The posters were like the ones we had seen at each of the three Cousin Carrie's we had visited. They all were reprints of the rave magazine review of the restaurant chain. The backgrounds of the posters were of different colors. Posters in one of the piles had a black background. The second pile contained red posters. The posters yet to be laminated sported a green background.

"I wonder why they're different colors," I questioned.

"There seem to be something else a little odd about them too," Sophie said. Before she was able to clarify that remark, we heard footsteps outside in the corridor. Sophie quickly pulled out her cell phone and took pictures of the top poster in each pile. As she snapped the final shot, the door to the office opened and Mrs. Gillespie stood there glaring at us. If ever there were a time for me to gulp, this was it.

Chapter 30

NOTE: THE FOLLOWING MONOLOGUE HAS been edited slightly to prevent it from receiving an X-rating:

"What the (Dickens) are you two (curious) (individuals) doing in my (private) office? (My goodness!), I remember you two (unusual looking) (personages): you're the two (adventurous) (people) from (sophisticated) New York, aren't you? You're the (children of unmarried parents) who snooped around at the (colorful) airport, aren't you? Are you the (mysterious) visitors who (very much) wanted to see me? There's no (possible) way that I'm going to waste any more of my (precious) time talking with you (delightful people). Now scram!"

At least the last injunction did not require any editing. It was short if not sweet and accompanied by the always controlled Mrs. Gillespie grabbing a baseball bat that somehow was handy and raising it menacingly in our direction. We scrammed.

We probably broke several world records arriving back at the restaurant's front desk. Lelia looked at us strangely, as Sophie muttered a number of choice epithets under her breath. To preclude that

X-rating I shall completely refrain from quoting her. I did suggest that we might lunch somewhere else less perilous and apologized to the hostess that we were forced to forgo luncheon here because something unforeseen had come up. I turned to vacate Cousin Carrie's when Sophie suddenly let out a yelp.

"Harry, I can't believe this. I left my tote bag in that harridan's office. All my notes, my phone, my wallet, everything is in that bag. We'll have to go back for it."

To my dying day I shall always be utterly ashamed that the following whispered words then escaped my lips: "WE have to go back for it?" Bert Lahr couldn't have spoken that humiliating line more convincingly.

Before a hole in the floor opened up to allow me mercifully to escape the tumult of Sophie's expected response, the waitress hurried up to us and said, "Mrs. Gillespie told me to bring this back to you. You must have left it behind."

It was the irreplaceable tote bag. Sophie made a cursory examination of its contents. Surprised, she said simply, "It looks like everything's here." Who says there are no such things as miracles?

We decided to drive back to the Magill house and have lunch there. I was feeling particularly tired and my headache was beginning to bother me again. The set-to with Mrs. Gillespie might have had something to do with the way I felt. Sophie advised me to take another nap after lunch to prep myself for the evening rehearsal. She said she had a great number of loose strings to review and pursue, and she hoped to get to many of them while I was asleep.

While we were enjoying the protein-rich feast Mrs. Donohue had quickly put together for us, Sophie emptied out her tote bag and assured herself that all items were present and accounted for. I was finishing my protein shake when I heard Sophie exclaim, "Why that miserable old (so-and-so)!" Sophie's colorful description of Mrs. Gillespie has been edited once again for a family audience. I gave her a questioning glance to which she replied, "The photos I took of the three posters have been deleted from my phone. She must have done that before she returned my bag. Now, I'm even more eager and determined to find out what's so odd about them."

I was incredulous. "You're not planning on risking another *contretemps* with that wild woman, are you?"

"No, I'm not quite that brave. But I think we can get a look at those posters without risking a felony charge or more busted skulls by sneaking into her office."

Before she could elucidate the details of her idea, her cell phone rang. "Hello, Barbara, how are you doing? That's good to hear. You do? That's great." Looking at me and noticing my attempt to stifle a mighty yawn, Sophie continued, "I tell you what, why don't I drive right over to your place and we can discuss your new bits of information and an idea that's just occurred to me. That way, the boss can get a little rest and quiet. Fine, I'll see you in a couple of minutes."

I wished Sophie happy hunting with Barbara Wright and trudged up the stairs to my bed where I conked out almost as soon as my bruised head connected with the pillow. The dream included dastardly dentists, old ladies swinging baseball bats, lavish yachts and exploding boats, an organ-playing Barbara seen from the back who turns around and is revealed to be her daughter Sally's pink diamond-studded cell phone held by her left hand marked with a copper-colored crescent moon, which morphs into Edward's hand which waves as he leaps off the observation deck. A clap of thunder woke me up.

As I entered the living room I saw that Sophie had just returned home and was removing a wet raincoat. "Do you see how fast it's coming down? How are you feeling, boss? Did you get some rest?

Would you like to hear my news now or would you rather get ready for dinner?" I didn't know which question to answer first, so I merely smiled and with a hand gesture suggested she proceed. We sat down on the sofa, and she removed her cell phone from her tote bag and displayed a picture on the view screen. It was a close-up of one of the restaurant review posters.

"You got one," I exclaimed.

"I got six of them." She displayed all the poster photos with a swipe of her finger and an air of satisfaction. "How do you like them apples, Dragon Lady!"

When I asked her how she had performed these marvels, she related her afternoon peregrinations: "When I arrived at Barbara's apartment, I told her that we had some questions about the woman who was the regional manager of the restaurant at the airport which Edward was accused of robbing. We also had some questions about her restaurant chain. Without revealing the details of our Bonnie and Clyde break-in of her office, I said there seemed to be something odd about the posters that were being printed at the main branch. She told me there were six Cousin Carrie branches around the area. I googled their addresses and asked Barbara if she would go to some of them and take clear photos of the posters. Although a little mystified, she said she would do anything we asked if it might lead to the truth and . . ."

"Yes, I know, Justice," I chimed in.

"Right. We divided them up by location and went our separate ways. As soon as she got to a restaurant, she found the poster and snapped a picture of it. She then immediately e-mailed the picture to my phone and left to go to the next one. To prevent another confrontation, I made sure Barbara went to the main branch and not I. We both successfully achieved our objectives. One thing I notice that's screwy about the different colored posters is they list different dates for the same review."

"I'm not sure I understand, Sophie."

"Look, here." She punched keys on her laptop. "This is the *New England Today* magazine's website. And here's the review of Cousin Carrie's Home Style Cooking. It clearly states the date of the review as November 18th of last year. Now let's look at the texts of the reviews printed in poster form. There are three different dates listed on them. All have the same year, but the month and day of the month are listed incorrectly."

"You said there were six branches, but only three deviations in the dates?"

"That's right, Harry. There are only three different colored backgrounds on the six posters. The two red ones list the date as May 22nd, the two black ones: March 11th, the two green ones: October 7th."

"This all seems crazy. Could they just be typographical errors?"

"I wouldn't think so, but who knows? Plus there seem to be other minor differences in the text of the review as well. But I'll need more time than I've had to give them the closer scrutiny required to work that out."

"You've done a masterful job, Sophie. By the way, didn't Barbara say on the phone that she had some information on her own for us?"

"That's right, I almost forgot. She heard back from some people she knew about a couple of less than respectable places in the area that Edward might have taken Sally to. The two they mentioned are rumored to have illegal gambling in their back rooms. One is the disco we already have on our list. The other one, are you ready for this, Harry, is The Copper Moon."

"Well, that seems to clinch it, Sophie. We definitely have to go there as soon as we can and do some major investigating."

"You betcha, boss."

"Sophie, I had a weird dream this afternoon. In it, among many other images, I believe I saw the Sea Witch tethered to a big yacht. I must have been thinking of the important client Billy Lee told us the Bensons went out on their boat to meet. I think it will be worth our time to find out the identity of that client. Who knows where that might lead?"

"That's a great idea, Harry. You know, I think I'll put in a call to Lieutenant Mossgrove, the Coast Guard guy who saved us when we were stranded in Tom's boat. He said he was a good friend of Tom and Barbara's. He might be willing to help us locate the yacht. Maybe I'll call Barbara right now and ask for her help in contacting him. She should be back home by now."

Let me digress a bit to mention the term synchronicity. Do you know it? It was first described by the Swiss psychologist Carl Gustav Jung in the 1920s I believe. It's the experience of two or more events as meaningfully related, even though they are unlikely to be causally related. A famous example: a French writer states in his memoirs that a stranger we'll call Monsieur X treated him to his first plum pudding. A decade later, the writer saw plum pudding listed on a restaurant menu. He wanted to order some, but the waiter told him the last dish had already been served to another customer, who turned out to be Monsieur X. Many years later, the writer was at a dinner and once again ordered plum pudding. He remembered the earlier incident and told his friends that only Monsieur X was missing to make the evening complete. Of course at that same moment, the gentleman in question entered the room.

So why do I take the time to discuss synchronicity? Actually, it is a way for me to delay describing the terrible event that happened next. Well, here goes. As Sophie reached for her phone to call Barbara

Wright, the phone rang in her hand. Answering it she said, "Why, it's Barbara. That's a coincidence." Or another example of synchronicty. But I am forced to return to the phone conversation.

"Barbara, I was just about to . . . What, Barbara? What's the matter? I can hardly understand you. Please slow down and try to stop crying. What, Barbara? . . . Oh, my God! We'll be right there, Barbara. We'll be right there."

"Sophie, what happened?" "Oh, Harry. Barbara just received a phone call from the police. They've found the body of a young woman. They think it's Sally."

Chapter 31

We shook out our wet umbrellas and left them outside the front door of the Wrights' apartment. Robby Donohue came over to us as we entered. "Barbara is lying down right now. The doctor's giving her something to help calm her down." His words were immediately refuted by a scream from the master bedroom: "No! I don't want to go to sleep! I have to make sure who it is. It's not Sally! It can't be! I have to go there and make sure who it is."

Barbara then ran into the living room followed by Ruth Catherine. She immediately saw us and made a mad dash to my side. "Harry, Harry, I know it can't be Sally. Make them let me see the body. I can tell them who it is. I'll know if it's my baby or not. Help me, Harry."

Robby quietly and calmly said, "Barbara, we've told you that the body was in such a condition that she can only be identified by forensic means. We've sent for her dental records. Until then, don't you think you'll be better able to deal with whatever we find if you're more rested?"

"Come now, Mrs. Wright," Ruth Catherine's voice was soothing and gentle. "What Officer Donohue is saying makes absolute sense. You've had a terrible shock, another terrible shock. Your system needs all the help it can get to cope. Please let me give you this to help you sleep for a little while. By then, the identification will be made. You'll be in a healthier place to deal with whatever we find if you're rested."

"Harry, what do you think?"

"Barbara, I think you should listen to Dr. Rodgers. She wants what's best for you. We all do. Please lie down. I promise you I'll find out the truth."

"And there will be justice?" she pleaded.

"I give you my word."

"All right," she turned to the doctor. "Please help me get some sleep." She took a few steps then turned back to me. "I know it's not Sally. I know it."

We watched Ruth Catherine lead poor Barbara to her bedroom then slowly sat down. Robby joined us and told us what he knew. The body of a drowned girl had been washed up on the shore a few miles away. The preliminary report stated that she had been in the water for several days. The body was so badly battered with such massive head trauma that visual identification was not possible.

"Was she murdered then?" Sophie's voice quavered a bit.

"There's no way of telling for sure right now. The injuries may very well have been caused after she drowned. A lot of forensic tests need to be conducted before any conclusions can be drawn."

"Why do you think it was Sally then?" I asked.

"The drowning victim had the same height, body type and hair coloring as Sally." He interrupted me from objecting by saying, "Of course that's certainly inconclusive. But there were some clothing and jewely remaining on the body. They matched the description her mother gave us of what Sally was wearing Saturday night when she disappeared."

A knock on the door then had our attention. The last person I wanted to see at that moment entered the apartment and strode up to Robby. "Here are the dental records for Sally Wright, as you demanded, officer. Obtaining them after office hours caused unnecessary difficulties. I'm sure you could have waited till morning."

"It was only a matter of life and death," Sophie muttered under her breath.

"Thank you, Doctor Ronchak," Robby quickly said. "We appreciate it."

"Humph" seems the closest phonetic approximation of the grunt uttered by Ruth Catherine's brother-in-law. "It's incomprehensible that such a charming woman could have produced such a boob as you, Officer Donohue." He glared at all three of us before rapidly leaving.

"Quite a sweetheart. Why did Robby call him Ronchak? Isn't his last name Rodgers too?" I whispered to Sally.

"No, I've googled both him and Dr. Rodgers. Ronchak was her husband's last name, but she uses her maiden name professionally."

When Ruth Catherine emerged from the bedroom a few minutes later, she told us that Barbara was now asleep and should remain so for several hours at least. "But is there someone who can stay here in case something unforeseen happens?"

"I'll stay with Barbara," Sophie quickly volunteered. "I know you'll want to go to the rehearsal, boss."

"Should we have one tonight considering everything?" I asked. "I wonder if we should even hold the memorial Thursday night."

"I think you should, Mr. Hunt," Robby said in a very serious tone. "This means a lot to all the actors, including me. They've all worked very hard and want to show how much they cared for Tom Wright and Noah and Nora Benson. And now, maybe, Sally. Whether or not

Barbara will be able to participate, it will mean the world to her and the whole village that the show will go on. We're all grieving, Mr. Hunt. We need to do something. And, I've got to hand it to you, you've put together a moving and beautiful evening. I hope you'll help us make it perfect. We need you at the last two rehearsals."

What could I say? Of course I agreed.

"I tell you what, Miss Xerxes," Robby continued. Why don't I call my mother and ask her to sit with Barbara so you can be at the rehearsal too? I'm sure she'll be happy to do it."

And that's what happened. Mrs. Donohue was over in a jiffy and even made some dinner for Sophie and me in Barbara's kitchen. The red Felix-the-cat-type clock with its moving eyes and tail seemed to cast a homey aura during the meal, and I felt a little better when the smiling cat showed it was time for us to go to Laurence House for the final rehearsal. Neither Robby nor Ruth Catherine shared our meal. He had immediately rushed out to fax the dental report to the hospital in the state capital. Ruth Catherine went home and said she'd look forward to seeing me after the rehearsal to begin the biofeedback exercise "finally." Sophie heard this last word, gave me a quizzical look, but said nothing. I also remained mum. Although I'm sure I blushed.

The Little Players and Miss Laurence were all shocked to hear why Barbara was not at rehearsal. The news of another death was horrible for them to hear. The possibility that the victim might be Sally made it almost unbearable. But they carried on like troupers. Robby even managed to make the last hour of the very successful rehearsal. In addition to helping me at the rehearsal, Sophie made some phone calls the results of which she recorded assiduously in her notebook. While we were all enjoying the traditional post-rehearsal tea (courtesy of Miss Laurence) and freshly baked pastries (courtesy of Mrs.

Donohue—tonight they were crumpets), Robby received a phone call. I walked over to him.

"Any news?" I quietly asked him.

He looked gravely at me, then *sotto voce* he said these terrible words: "This is just between us, Mr. Hunt. The dental records seem to match. Further forensic work needs to be done, but the initial findings seem to indicate that it's Sally."

Forty minutes later, I was once again lying on the settee in Ruth Catherine's library. Hearing that it was very likely that Sally had been found, I more than ever needed to master this relaxation technique. The electrical sensors were once again attached to my head. They in turn were connected to a monitor which displayed, as Ruth Catherine put it, my body's physiological state, such as brain waves, skin temperature or muscle tension. The information was fed back to me via two cues: a beeping sound and a flashing light. My goal was to learn from the feedback how to change or control my body's physiological reactions, the tense muscles causing the headaches, by changing my thoughts, emotions, and that sort of thing.

It was really difficult at first to affect that beeping tone at all, but with the soothing, supportive advice and suggestions made by Ruth Catherine, the damn process started to work. I seemed to be able to reduce the tension a bit with my thoughts. It was an amazing, empowering sensation.

Also helping my relaxation was the presence of her sweet dog Roscoe who delighted in lying on the floor next to me as I softly petted him. Ruth Catherine told me about the recent research that pets can improve our physical well-being. A former hospital president is so convinced of the healing powers of pets that he actually prescribed them for one third of his cancer patients. She said that the simple act of petting a dog results in a drop in blood pressure. A study showed that owning a pet blunted the blood pressure response to mental stress while the traditionally prescribed hypertension drug did not.

Ruth Catherine left Roscoe and me to our own devices after I seemed to catch on to the process. She said she had some files to go over and would come back to the library in a half hour or so. About ten minutes after she left, I heard the soft sound of the light rain outside the window change to a steady downpour. I noticed as well that Roscoe was becoming a little agitated. This seemed to suggest that another thunderstorm was imminent. Suddenly, Roscoe began to panic. The door to the library had been left open a jot, and the poor dog sped out of the room like a rocket. I detached myself from the sensors and followed him into the downstairs bathroom.

Roscoe was trying desperately to wedge himself into the tiniest space he could find. As he manically adjusted his position time after time, he knocked against a low cupboard and somehow caused the cupboard door to open. As he rubbed back and forth attempting to hide in one of the open shelves, several objects were dislodged and fell to the floor. I petted Roscoe with one hand in an attempt to calm him down a little. With the other hand I managed to pick up a fallen jar of medicated ointment and replace it in the cupboard. My hand touched something cold and made of metal. It felt like . . . . Was that possible? Holding the dog still with one hand, I removed the object from the back of the shelf. It was a gun.

CHAPTER 32

YES, A GUN. AND NOT a sweet, lady-like, stylish, pearl-handled derringer that a sweet, lady-like, stylish angel of mercy (who would never willingly hurt a fly) might be prevailed upon to keep on her premises strictly for self-protection purposes only. No, this gun was a very heavy, very dangerous-looking, high-caliber killing machine that would only be owned by someone who definitely meant business, like a mobster, a gangster or (it was impossible not to think of it) a murderer. Oh, my heavens. Also hidden in the back of that shelf were a professional, mean looking leather holster and several boxes of cartridges.

The rumblings of thunder that only Roscoe could sense had apparently abated as he noticeably relaxed and licked my hand. Since this was the hand that still held the revolver, I quickly but carefully replaced the gun in the cupboard so that no sign of my tampering could be detected. I hoped.

Roscoe and I returned to the library. Reattaching the sensors, I tried to do that biofeedback trick once again. If ever I needed to relax, it was now. But my thoughts were too chaotic and frantic to even bother.

So, I called Ruth Catherine's name and when she returned told her I had enough of the procedure for today and bade her goodnight. That delicious smile appeared again, but this time it had less of an effect on me.

The heavy rain was now only a drizzle as I walked home, but I barely noticed. What did the presence of that arsenal in Ruth Catherine's Laura Ashleyesque powder room portend if anything? I remembered the blatant lie that she had told me last night. What was that all about? Who really was this Dr. Rodgers? Did she have a secret identify like the members of the Justice League or rather their archenemies the dastardly Secret Society of Super Villains (or the SSoSV)? I learned this valuable nugget of pop culture trivia from Sophie of course. Speaking of Sophie, what will I say to her about all this? Or should I say anything at all until I was more certain of the facts? As I entered the Magill home, I had not decided what to do.

Sophie was so full of information when I entered the living room that I wouldn't have been able to bring up my concerns about Dr. Rodgers even if I had wanted to.

"Harry, I'm so glad you finally got here. I've gotten a lot done. I remembered that Billy Lee Baxter had told us that Noah Benson, and I quote from my notes: 'he called me at the last minute and told me he and Nora were going to meet with an important customer on his yacht and didn't need me to come along. They did this every few months or so . . .' So, I called Billy Lee and asked him if he could remember exactly when they had taken the boat out to rendezvous with this unnamed yacht owner. He checked the logs of the Sea Witch and called me back. There were six times in the last two years. I then reached Lieutenant Mossgrove and told him we were helping Barbara Wright and, as a favor to her, would he provide us with the names of any yachts that were anchored not too far from Havenport this weekend and on the dates Billy Lee provided. It seemed forever before he called me back, but he finally did." She paused dramatically.

"Well, what did he tell you?" I practically screamed. "I'm on *shpilkes!*"

She looked at me with a puzzled expression. "That's Yiddish for 'pins and needles."

"I wasn't aware that you knew Yiddish," she said.

"There's a lot about me that you don't know. Now get on with it!"

"The Coast Guard's logs reported a number of yachts in nearby waters from time to time, but only one was here on all those dates including Sunday night. It's a very fancy number called the Jade Pebble. And it's still here."

"Sophie, I've never seen any large yachts since we've been in Havenport."

"Apparently, they're anchored many miles out in deep water."

"Did he say what he knows about the yacht's owners?"

"Only that they have plenty of money and have never caused the slightest trouble. They follow all safety and maritime rules and regulations and are strictly above board. He also told me that the Coast Guard and state police have no doubts that the Sea Witch's explosion was completely accidental and the result of an electric spark igniting gas fumes, exactly as Billy Lee hypothesized. There is absolutely no evidence of foul play. They'll make their decision known in a couple of days."

"Well, that doesn't sound too promising, does it?"

"Should I do more checking on the yacht's owners? See what connection they had with the Bensons?"

"It certainly wouldn't hurt. But I think we should give our primary attention to finding out what happened to Sally. It seems most likely that it was she who drowned. We need to uncover the particulars. How and why did she drown? Did it occur after her date with Edward, or, if we accept the police's theory, during it?"

"That makes sense, boss. So we go to The Copper Moon, I presume?"

"Yes, 'a trip to the moon on gossamer wings' seems to be in order. Maybe we can get into their infamous back room. How are your gambling skills?"

"I'll be better able to concentrate on them if you can guarantee not running into that charming Mrs. Gillespie who more than likely will be right next door."

"With that thought, my dear Sophie, I bid you goodnight. Bedtime for you too?"

"Nope not yet. There are so many unresolved mysteries to solve, I'll probably still be up to see that morning bird poor Barbara mentions in her sonnet."

"Ah, yes, I quoted:

> Haply I think on thee, and then my state,
> (Like to the lark at break of day arising
> From sullen earth) sings hymns at heaven's gate.

"Did you hear, Sophie, how brilliantly the Bard imitates in sound the way the lark, the most English of birds, flies almost vertically high up in the sky like a helicopter. The first and third lines I just quoted each consists of ten syllables—five two syllable feet—forming an almost perfect iambic pentameter meter. A good place to take a short breath is at the end of a punctuated pentameter line. In English we give a downward inflection at the end of a completed thought indicated by a punctuation mark. Every actor in Shakespeare's company would know that. But the middle line is an exception.

Like to the lark at break of day arising is unpunctuated and consists of eleven syllables. This is a clue from Shakespeare the director that the speaker not pause at the end of the unpunctuated line but rather carry the eleventh syllable along and continue it with one breath and an upward inflection until he reaches the next end stop or period after 'heaven's gate.'

> "... the lark at break of day arising
> /from sullen earth ...

therefore is spoken without taking a breath and with an upward inflection on 'arising' linking that word with the next line The sound imitates the rising motion of the bird. That man was a genius."

"Good night, Harry."

I stopped on the stairs. "Also, the upward inflection is actually given to the word 'arising' mimicking the meaning of the word in sound. Pure genius!"

"Pleasant dreams," said Sophie only rolling her eyes a little.

Chapter 33

Ruth Catherine was flying vertically aiming a rifle at a lark which swooped down onto a fancy yacht that exploded causing the lark to fly up once again and then land on the head of Edward who also flew down shouting, "Sally, I'll join you" to a drowned body before his head was smashed by a baseball bat-wielding Mrs. Gillespie. Thankfully, I awoke at that moment.

I wished Sophie good morning in the living room where she was perched over her laptop and then asked if she had gone to bed at all last night.

"Yes, I did, thank you. But I spent a lot of time last night going over my notes. I'll get to that in a minute. But I just checked The Copper Moon's website. They are usually only open for brunch on the weekend, but during the months of June and July they also feature a Wednesday afternoon brunch and jam session. They must get a lot of extra business from summer tourists."

"It would appear that we shall be two of those tourists this afternoon."

"I think that would be a very good plan. But I think I should be the only one of us in there, Harry. Remember how important it is for you to get your rest. If gambling goes on in their back rooms, maybe I can get in there and ask some questions. What I know about casinos is that the action is fast and furious all day and all night."

"Sophie, I appreciate your concern about my health, but I insist on visiting The Copper Moon today as well. I promise not to exert myself."

Seeing the determined look in my eye, Sophie was forced to cave. "All right, if you promise. Now let me show you what I've discovered in my notes. I've carefully gone over the lists of items I noticed in the trash receptacles at the airport."

"Something of interest?"

"Two things, actually. Remember those two cleaning women we saw? I believe their head scarves and uniforms had been deposited in the laundry bin located outside the employees' changing rooms. I didn't thing anything about that at the time."

"However, we've subsequently found out there is no record of female cleaners on the airport personnel records. So, what do we make of that?"

"What indeed?" Also the only other curious thing I found was that among the very few items in the V.I.P. lounge's wastebasket were two small paper envelopes slit open on the top. They were about the size of individual packs of sugar or artificial sweeteners. I don't think there was writing on the envelopes. But each was a different color. One was red and one was green. What makes this curious is that there was another one of these opened envelopes in the employees' laundry bin. Only this one was black."

"Red, green, and black. They're the same colors on the background of the restaurant review posters." Another bizarre mystery I couldn't solve, at least not yet. I was pretty bewildered.

"Speaking of those dang posters, I've made no headway in finding why there are discrepancies in the dates and text. But I'll keep working on it," Sophie said dejectedly. "Oh, also, Mrs. Donohue called a few minutes ago. She spent the night at Barbara's place. Barbara just woke up and according to Mrs. Donohue appears to be in better shape. She called Dr. Rodgers who said she would come over to check on Barbara shortly. I told her we would go over there after breakfast, but Mrs. Donohue wouldn't hear of it. She said she'd make breakfast for us at Barbara's."

"Well, what's stopping us? Let's go," I said with feigned heartiness. I didn't know how I felt about seeing Ruth Catherine this morning. Would she be toting her six-shooter?

We walked up the stairs from the general store and knocked. Barbara let us in. She certainly looked like the good night sleep had been most beneficial. She led us into the kitchen where Mrs. Donohue was performing her culinary magic. We all sat down to eat. I didn't want to be the one to tell Barbara that Sally's dental records seemed to match the corpse. So, instead I started talking about the first thing that came into my mind. "That cute Felix-the cat-like wall clock is similar to the one in the Bensons' kitchen, only this one is red. I've seen many of these types of clocks in the village. Where did they all come from?"

Barbara answered: "A number of years ago the man who rented the Magill house gave them all to us as presents. He imports them I understand, and he wanted to make a good impression on the villagers. I guess he wanted us to say a good word about him to Madge, so that she'd be more inclined to sell the house to him. But it didn't work. When her parents died, she absolutely wanted to keep the house until she could move in full time. The clocks come in a variety of styles and colors. Sally has a black one in her bedroom. It was surprising that she didn't pick a pink one since that's her favorite color. You have one too in your room, don't you Edna?"

"That's right," said Mrs. Donohue. "I'm very partial to little Felix. Mine is black too."

"I wouldn't mind one of those in my place. It certainly would brighten up my kitchen," Sophie said. "What's the man's name?"

"It's Greenleaf, I think, or something like that. Edna, you'd know. You kept house for him when he rented it each year."

"Greenstone. Henry Greenstone. And a very nice, convivial gentleman he is."

"He has plenty of money I guess. During the summers he comes every now and then and lives on his pretty impressive looking yacht. Tom took me past it several times on his boat. Very nice."

Sophie and I looked at each other. Just then, Ruth Catherine knocked on the door. She took Barbara into the bedroom to examine her. When they returned to the kitchen, the doctor seemed pleased. "I'm leaving you some sleeping pills to take for the next few nights whenever you're not able to sleep, Barbara. You've been through quite a trauma. Oh, Harry, I've brought a portable biofeedback device for you. Since you seem to be getting the hang of it, you can simply attach it to the USB port of a computer and work on it at your own pace." I took the package and thanked her. I believe my remark did not come out as warmly as I had intended. She looked at me a bit strangely but didn't comment.

Sophie's phone rang at that moment. "It's Madge," she said to us. After a minute or two she responded, "That's really good news, Madge. We'll see you this afternoon."

"What did she say?" I asked.

"Edward has come out of his coma. Of course he's still highly sedated. But the doctors hope he may be able to speak some time late this afternoon."

"How wonderful," Mrs. Donohue exclaimed. "I've prayed for nothing less."

"Very good news, indeed," the doctor said with a smile. She looked at her watch.

"Well, I'm on my way to the medical center now. I'm so delighted about Edward and about how well you're doing, Barbara. Are you going to the hospital now?" she asked Sophie and me.

"Madge said there wouldn't be anything new to report until four or five o'clock. Harry and I have a lot of finishing touches to do on the memorial before the final rehearsal tonight, and then we're going to treat ourselves to a fancy brunch, so you're excused this afternoon, Mrs. Donohue."

"Where will you be going?" Ruth Catherine asked.

"A place we've heard good things about, The Copper Moon."

The doctor gave us the strangest look and said rather sharply, "No, you don't want to go there, Harry. I've been there once and I was very disappointed. I suggest the Crab and Lobster on the state road. It's much better."

"Well, all right. We'll take your advice, thank you," I said.

"Good." She looked again at her watch. "Well, I'll see you all soon," she said as she left.

"I'd like to go to the hospital with you to check the body, Harry. I'll be calm, don't worry. But I just know in my bones that it can't be Sally."

"We'll call you this afternoon, Barbara. Try to get a little more rest."

"I will, Sophie, thanks."

"See you all later then." And Sophie and I quickly left.

In the car, I asked Sophie to try and follow the doctor as she was only a couple of minutes ahead of us. "I'm concerned about her vehement reaction to our going to The Copper Moon."

"That certainly seemed odd I must admit."

"And I need to tell you some other odd things about Dr. Rodgers."

"Oh?" Sophie gave me a questioning glance. "Oh, look, there's her van. We'll stay a safe distance from her. Why do you want to follow her?"

"I have the strangest hunch that she's not going to her medical center."

"Oh really? Very well. 'Lead on, Macduff.'"

"That's a common misquote by the way, Sophie. The actual line is "Lay on, Macduff, and damned be him who first cries: Hold enough!'"

"I'm completely chastened, Harry, now spill your guts about the lady doctor."

CHAPTER 34

I SPILLED ALL MY GUTS, as Sophie so elegantly put it. She didn't say anything for a few moments. Then, "So, you think she lied to you about how she learned the Sea Witch had exploded."

"I know she lied, Sophie."

"Hmmm." She was silent for another few moments. "How can you be sure the gun is hers and not that nasty Basil Ronchak's?"

"He lives on the second floor and has his own separate apartment with its own bathroom. She and the dog live on the first floor. If he were going to hide weapons, it seems unlikely that he would do so in a cupboard in her bathroom."

"Hmmm." Another pause. "She did seem a little on edge today. Hmmm."

"Enough with all those sounds of deep introspection, if you don't mind, Sophie!" I exploded.

In a calm, rational voice Sophie then quoted Hamlet perfectly," There is nothing either good or bad but thinking makes it so."

I looked at her with astonishment. "Bravo, my dear Sophie."

She acknowledged my accolade with a regal nod then quickly said," Look, she's nearing the turnoff for the medical center."

We watched in silence as she stayed on the state road and passed the cineplex at one end of the mall and the medical center at the other without turning.

"I guess I'm not the only one full of little surprises today, Harry. Your hunch seems to be right. So where is she going?"

There was no way of answering that question, so we continued to follow the van at a safe distance. I soon brought up another confusing subject. "What are we to make of the fact that the person who rented Madge's house during the school year for a number of years is also the owner of the yacht we think the Bensons might have visited? Is it simply a colossal coincidence, a red herring that fate has thrown in our path as one great cosmic joke, or is there something fishy about this whole thing?"

"There's something fishy all right, but it's not that herring. There must be some connection. Uh oh! Our lady doctor just signaled that she'll be turning . . ."

"Into the parking lot for either Cousin Carrie's Home Style Cooking or The Copper Moon," I finished her sentence. Which do you think is her destination?"

"Considering how strongly she tried to convince us not to go to The Copper Moon, I would think that's the stronger candidate."

"Not having to face Jessie Gillespie wouldn't have anything to do with your decision, would it?" I laughed.

"You might have a point." We also made the turn. "Well, she's parked near the jazz club. I'll park on the other side."

We watched as Dr. Rodgers entered The Copper Moon. "Let's wait a few minutes and then take our chances and follow her in." There may have been an inadvertent gulp or two in my delivery of that line.

The interior of the club was quite attractive, the lights were pleasantly dimmed and the music from the small combo surprisingly good. We paid the $20 cover charge and had the back of our left hands stamped with that all so familiar crescent moon. It gave me an odd feeling whenever I happened to look at it. We were told that the cover charge would apply to this evening as well. We were seated at a small table near the left wall but still not too far from the bandstand and were given food and beverage menus.

"Do you see her?" I whispered to Sophie.

"No, I don't. Oh, there, she's just come out of the ladies' room and now is . . . duck!"

I followed Sophie's lead and hid my face in the menu. Our eyes slowly were raised over the top of our menus and we saw Dr. Rodgers walk up to a door well hidden in the very dimly lit back wall and knocked three times. In a moment, the door opened a crack and she was admitted inside. The door quickly closed behind her. We couldn't make out anything about the interior room.

"I wonder if the owners of this place were fans of *Pajama Game*?" I said then softly sang:

> Just knock three times and whisper low
> That you and I were sent by Joe.
> Then strike a match and you will know
> You're in Hernando's Hideaway . . ."

Before I could warble the climactic "Olé," Sophie shushed me. "I know how you miss Carol Haney, Harry, but please keep it down. So should we try to get in that den of iniquity now, wait for the good doctor to leave and then go in, or none of the above?"

"Hello, my name is Veronica, and I'll be your server. May I take your drink order?" The attractive woman with very long legs displayed in a very short skirt smiled at us.

"Actually, uh, Veronica," I improvised. "We were to meet a friend here but we don't see her. Is there another room where she might be?"

"Another room?"

"Yes," I answered with what I hoped was a knowing, sophisticated air. I took out a $5 dollar bill and placed it in front of the server. "A more private room?"

"Uh, let me check. I'll be right back." She snatched the money and walked to a small telephone located near the entrance. We couldn't hear what she said, but soon the door in the back opened and two rather scary-looking men came over to our table. They looked more like credible cast replacements for *The Sopranos* than I would have imagined could be found on the rocky New England shore, but they weren't actors. They were real. And they were here leaning over us.

"We hear you're looking for some sort of a private room," Gangster one snarled at me.

"Yes, that's right. A place where we might enjoy some sort of rollicking gaming action perhaps?"

"You're in the wrong place, buddy," growled Gangster two grabbing my collar. In less than a minute I had been lifted off the ground by the two of them and deposited ungracefully in the parking lot with my bones intact but my self-respect crushed. Sophie had run as quickly as she could behind us and had been a witness to my less than dignified exit. She said, "Rollicking gaming action? That was what you came up with?"

"I'm doing the best I can," I said dejectedly.

"I know you are, Harry, and maybe this will make you feel a little better." It was so dark in there, I only noticed these as . . . we left. They were in a container on our table. "She held up a half dozen packs of sugar. They matched the description of the open envelopes she had noted at the airport. Two were red, two were green, and two were black.

"So, what's so unusual about empty sugar packs? Maybe a customer of this place took some packs of sugar with him to the airport and used them in a cup of coffee."

"Maybe. Or maybe there's another reason," she added cryptically.

I called Madge from the parking lot. She said that it would be all right for us to talk to Edward if and when he regained consciousness. She had verified this with the police officer guarding his room. She told us he was in a special closed wing, room 766. I told her we would go to the hospital now and would speak to her when we got there. I then called Barbara. I told her we were half way to the hospital now and would she mind meeting us there. She agreed and told us she had been given permission by the police medical team at the morgue in the hospital to examine the body to see if she could identify whether or not it was her daughter. "They told me the body is so disfigured and battered by its time in the ocean that I probably wouldn't be able to help. But, Harry, I'll know whether or not it's Sally. I'll know whether or not it's my baby." I told her to call Sophie or me when she arrived at the hospital. We would most likely already be there.

Sophie typed the name of the hospital into the GPS, and Manderville directed us there without any complications. I must say my previous antipathy to this helpful electronic mapping device now seemed rather foolish. In about 40 minutes we arrived at the hospital. I hadn't been in a hospital since I was detained briefly in the one in Brookfield. I had also visited Belinda there. I thought about Belinda. How strong were my feelings for her if I had so easily been attracted by Ruth Catherine. Well, that was over now I was happy to say. And

I would know for sure how I felt about Belinda when I saw her in London next month.

But I was now in the lobby of this larger hospital in the state capital not too far away from the airport where I had watched Edward leap from the observation deck. Now I would be seeing him once again and I hoped would be able to speak to him. What would he tell us? When the nurse at the front desk heard the room number, she gave us a suspicious look. But when she saw that our names were on the approved visitor list, she gave us each an identification tag and told us to present them to Officer Krupke when we got to room 766. She seemed confused when Sophie and I both grinned like madmen when we heard the name.

It was a little tricky locating the closed wing despite the directions the nurse had given us. We could have used Manderville to help us out. However, after a few wrong turns we found ourselves in the right place and took the elevator to the seventh floor. Every room we passed was empty. Edward was a murder suspect and was secluded from the general population of the hospital. Finally we found room 766. The door was closed. We expected to find a unformed policeman guarding the door. But, curiously, the corridor was empty.

"I may be crazy, Harry, but I'm not feeling good about this," Sophie whispered.

"Let's think only good thoughts," I whispered back. Besides, Madge will more than likely be in there at Edward's bedside. I opened the door. Strangely the room was dark. It looked like the shades had been drawn. We saw the shadowy figure of someone standing above Edward's bed. But it was too tall to be Madge, and the figure was holding a pillow and squeezing it over Edward's face.

The lights switched on and a woman's voice shouted, "Hold it right there!" All three of us immediately turned around and faced the speaker. It was Ruth Catherine Rodgers. She pointed a gun at us and shouted once more, "I said hold it!" Simultaneously, Sophie and I raised our arms. Were we now to be killed? The figure behind us threw the pillow he was holding at Ruth Catherine. The gun was knocked from her hand onto the floor. And then a man's voice cried out from the bed, "She said hold it!" The man who had attempted to smother Edward reached for his own gun, and then Edward (Could it be Edward?) used his own weapon to shoot twice. The man behind us groaned and fell. For the first time we were now able to identify the face of the man lying unconscious on the floor. It was Robby Donohue.

"So who are you again," I asked quite bewildered.

She smiled and patiently repeated, "I'm Special Agent Ruth Catherine Rodgers of the D.E.A."

"D.E.A.? That's Dance Educators of America. Sophie, remember we appeared at a fundraising event for them. You're a dance teacher with a gun?"

"D.E.A. is also an acronym for the Drug Enforcement Administration. It's a federal agency under the Department of Justice. Our job is combating drug smuggling within the United States and coordinating and pursuing U.S. drug investigations abroad."

"So, you're not a doctor?"

"Yes, Harry, I'm also an M.D. What I've told you about myself is all true. But there's more. Let me tell you the whole story."

And so she did. Ruth Catherine Rodgers Ronchak lived in suburban Maryland with her husband and ten year old son. She enjoyed her flourishing medical practice. Although her husband displayed occasional mood swings, their relationship seemed pretty solid. Everything changed a few years ago when her husband's brother, a dentist from Havenport, made his annual visit. Basil, his brother, and nephew drove off one morning to go to a baseball game in Washington. Basil had driven. There was a car crash. Her husband died instantly; her son died days later. Although severely injured, her brother-in-law was the only survivor. It was determined that Basil and her husband had a substantial amount of drugs in their bloodstream.

It was then that Ruth Catherine made a life-changing decision. She applied to be an agent of the D.E.A. After a rigorous training course, her first case involved the drug cartel that had ultimately provided the illegal substances that Basil had obtained. He now was desperately trying to stay off drugs. He had never been a sunny person, but now the intense guilt he experienced for his relatives' deaths coupled with the one-day-at-a-time struggle to stay clean resulted in the Mister Conviviality we had oh so enjoyed meeting. He allowed her to move into his house and take over the medical center in which he had his practice. Although he would never be allowed to join the agency, he did help in this way.

"But why Havenport?" I asked.

"Right," said Sophie. "I thought drugs were smuggled through Florida. That's where all the busts are made, right?"

"This area of New England has become a major rival to Florida as the favorite destination of drug smugglers from South America and the Caribbean. In fact, it's the recent federal pressure on smuggling into Florida that may be the cause of increased activity here. Drug-carrying ships can evade our ships and planes guarding access routes to Florida by sailing hundreds of miles east from South American ports before turning north toward New England. In doing so, their arrival time off the New England coast is still only two days later than it would be if they sailed straight to Florida, Using the cover of commercial and pleasure boat traffic, the drugs are then ferried ashore. And we do see an increase in the number of local people making their living in drug trafficking." Ruth Catherine paused to let all this sink in.

Then I asked again, "But WHY Havenport?" My vocal delivery was apparently so comical that Sophie and Ruth Catherine both broke up. It was a needed tension-breaker.

She continued, "Our international colleagues suggested we keep our eyes out for a man who might have Colombian drug connections. He often sails his yacht near here and in the past he has rented a house in Havenport."

Sophie and I shouted out the name "Henry Greenstone" at the same time making quite a clamor. It was fortunate there were no patients on this floor of the hospital wing. The severely wounded Robby Donohue had been removed to another floor by Officer Krupke and other state policemen. It had been he who had masqueraded as Edward Magill and had shot Robby to protect all of us. Ruth Catherine had told us that the D.E.A. had prevailed upon Madge to spread the ruse that Edward had come out of his coma and might be able to speak today in the hope that an attempt would be made to prevent that from happening. Edward's actual room was on another floor. Sadly, he remained in a coma. We would visit him and Madge shortly.

"So you know about Henry Greenstone too? You both amaze me. You should be conducting this investigation, not me." I assumed that Ruth Catherine was joking when she made this remark. Sophie looked as if she agreed with the special agent.

"So why did you think Edward was somehow involved in all of this?" Sophie vocalized my confusion as well.

"There was the same type of hallucinogenic drug in Edward's system that this cartel specializes in. It was a miracle that he survived the fall. If he had died, it would obviously have been declared a suicide and likely no further investigation would have been made. However, there were too many other bizarre occurrences (Sally's disappearance, her father's murder, the assault on the restaurant manager, and then the Bensons' deaths) that nagged at me."

"Of course, all good detectives would think that way," Sophie almost gloated as she said this.

"Robby is involved in this whole thing then?"

"It appears so, Harry. But much more work is needed to connect all the dots. We do know that Basil gave Sally's dental records to Robby. However, when they were faxed to the forensic people, other records had been substituted that did match the dead body."

"How do you know that?"

"Because I told them, Harry." We turned to see that a uniformed cop had directed Barbara Wright to the little waiting room in which we were seated. She continued, "I had requested Dr. Ronchak send me a copy of her records when I first began searching for Sally. I thought they might come in handy. I brought them with me today, and they were obviously not the ones the doctors here had been working with. I went directly to the morgue when I got here." Barbara had calmly said these words. It was clear that she was much, much better physically and emotionally.

Ruth Catherine went on with the timeline, "Forensics called me that moment and I went immediately up to room 766 after I saw that Robby Donohue had logged in. I got there just in time to see his attempt to smother the man he thought was Edward."

"Dear, Officer Krupke," I half sung and half chuckled.

"Yes, I love *West Side Story* too, and the coincidence in the names really is very funny." That wonderful smile made its appearance again. There was a lot to like about Ruth Catherine Rodgers.

"Now that I've made a clean breast of my secret identity, I want to hear all your theories on this case. They're probably superior to mine."

And, ye gods, was Sophie happy to oblige. As she did so, it occurred to me that the true member of the Justice League of America was not I but was in fact Ruth Catherine. I wager she would be more than proficient at spinning that lasso of truth, or whatever it's called.

"I'm intrigued and I'm afraid mystified by the constant references to red, green and black. You say these are the newest versions of the three slightly different posters?"

"Yes, we saw them in the process of being printed yesterday afternoon."

"I'll forward these pictures of yours to experts on code breaking, but, if you have time, Sophie, I'd like you to continue working with them too. You seem to have quite a facility for this sort of thing."

"Of course. Thank you, uh, may I call you Ruth Catherine?"

Look who just became BFFs. Who would have thought? Ruth Catherine then answered our question that Edward's fingerprints were not found in the airport Cousin Carrie's, and then told Sophie she'd have someone pick up the plastic bags of muddy, sandy substances she collected at the airport's VIP lounge to be "sent to the lab for testing."

All of us then went up to the eighth floor and visited Edward's room. Madge was sitting next to the bed holding his left hand. The ink mark there had almost completely faded I noticed. The one stamped on my hand (as well as Sophie's and Ruth Catherine's) was still quite bright despite my attempts to wash the damned thing off. Ruth Catherine had told us that Greenstone possibly was connected with The Copper Moon as well. She had put on a "wire" (I was surprised I knew what that term meant) in the club's ladies' room before she had entered the back room. The proof she obtained of the illegal gambling that took place there would be sent to the proper authorities in due time.

My heart went out to poor Edward lying there unconscious connected to so many tubes and machines. I felt equal sympathy for Madge who had always been so kind and hospitable to us. She turned to see that Ruth Catherine was with us. "Hello, Harry and Sophie. You see, Agent, I told you God's deputy would help all of us."

"It seems you were right, Madge." That smile again. I didn't know which way to look.

"This has been some tough day for all of us," Ruth Catherine said as the three of us left Madge sitting at Edward's side. "I advise you all get some rest. That is especially directed at you, Harry. You're still not absolutely out of the woods with that concussion, you know." I nodded. "You're going to a rehearsal for the memorial tonight, is that right? Then, please, don't say anything at all about what has happened to Robby. I've texted his mother using his cell phone telling her he had to go out of town on police business. I hope she believes the message came from him. If so, she'll probably tell you that he won't be at rehearsal tonight."

At the hospital parking lot, we said goodbye to Barbara. She said, "I'll see you at rehearsal tonight. I feel so confident that we'll find Sally and find her alive too. Soon. Maybe she'll be able to attend the memorial to her father tomorrow night. I want it to be perfect for her." She mouthed the words "thank you" to Sophie and me, blew us a kiss and then drove away.

When we got to the Magill house, Mrs. Donohue did deliver the message she said she received from Robby. "I hope he'll be back in time for the performance tomorrow night," she added. "It would be a shame if he had to miss it. He's such a good actor, you know."

One of the best I've ever met, I angrily thought to myself.

Chapter 36

It was Thursday. Tonight the memorial would be held six days after Tom Wright's murder. Six of the worst days of my life. At least I was as sure as I could be that this would go well. Dress rehearsal went beautifully last night. Everyone was sorry Robby couldn't be there but delighted to see Barbara. I had never heard her piece read so well. Moving and truthful and loving and heartbreaking. Sophie had worked on her laptop during the rehearsal trying to decipher that code, if in fact there were one. After we got home, she kept at it. She had printed out the pictures of the posters so I could take the laptop upstairs. I said goodnight and told her not to work too hard. She didn't answer, so engrossed was she in this frustrating labor.

In bed, I attached the biofeedback sensors to the laptop and to my skull in the manner I had been shown. It took a little time before I had relaxed enough to cause the beeping tone to change pitch. But finally it did. I let my thoughts float free and remembered many things. Suddenly I realized that two of them were highly important and were memories I had totally forgotten. I fell asleep thinking how happy Sophie would be to hear about these lost memories.

When I came downstairs, I asked Mrs. Donohue where Sophie was. "Oh, Mr. Hunt, good morning. Miss Sophie was up earlier than I was. She seemed very excited and told me there were things she had to do immediately. I forced her to have a small breakfast at least and was pleased she took the time to have a toasty hot toddy. It's gotten quite chilly again and it looks ready for a downpour. This is some June, right, Mr. Hunt?"

"One for the record books," I replied. "Did she leave a message for me, Mrs. Donohue?"

"Nothing in writing. But she said she'd call you as soon as she could. Would you like one of my famous hot toddies with your breakfast? It'll do you a world of good."

"I'll pass on the toddy, thank you anyway, and only a very small breakfast. I've got quite a bit to do today as well."

I dialed Sophie's cell phone but only reached her voice mail. I left a message for her to call me when she was able. I wondered where she went. Breakfast was of course delicious and the hot toddy Mrs. Donohue suggested again probably would have helped relax me, but I didn't need to relax now. I needed to work. Where was Sophie? Why hadn't she called?

"Good morning, Ruth Catherine, how are you? Good. Good. Yes it was a hectic day yesterday, yes. Listen, did Sophie call you? No? Mrs. Donohue says she left early this morning rather excited and said she'd call me when she could. But she hasn't. Yes, I'm sure she will. If you hear from her, please ask her to call me. Thanks. Yes, I'm sure there's no need for concern. Yes. Well, goodbye."

"Hello, Ruth Catherine, it's Harry again. I know it's only been an hour since I called you, but I still haven't heard from Sophie and I'm a bit worried. I keep getting her voice mail. And now Mrs. Donohue doesn't seem to be around. And I'm more than a bit worried. No, that's very nice of you, but I don't think there's any need for you to take the time and come over here, unless you really want to. You will. Oh, great. Thank you. See you soon."

I surprised myself and I think her by hugging Ruth Catherine when she arrived shortly after my second phone call. I got a little wet from putting my arms around her raincoat. I thanked her again and said this was so unlike Sophie to leave and not tell me where she was going. I asked her if she'd like something to eat or drink as we walked to the kitchen. Still no Mrs. Donohue. I called her name, but once again there was no response.

"Mrs. Donohue's car is the only one parked outside," Ruth Catherine said. "I suppose she could have walked downtown to do some shopping, but it's pretty wet outside. Let's go see if we can find her. Come on, it will put your mind at rest. And I'd like to ask her some questions about Henry Greenstone."

There was no answer when we knocked at the door to her room. We looked in. It was empty. "That's one more of those clocks everyone seems to have gotten from Greenstone, isn't it?"

"That's right. I find them cleverly nostalgic *albeit* a mite campy. This one is black like the one in the Benson kitchen." For the first time I sensed something a little ominous in that fact.

Ruth Catherine went over to the clock. Felix's eyes and tail moved with each passing second. She held the tail still and the eyes stared in place as well. The tail was apparently the pendulum of the clock. She took out a little penlight flashlight from her pocket and looked around the interior. I thought of Sophie. "There seems to be a little button right inside here," she said. "I wonder what it's there for." She must have pushed the button, for suddenly a little compartment snapped open.

"Well, would you look at that? Aren't these the colored sugar packets you've mentioned?" She held a red and a green one in her hand. They were sealed.

"There's also a black sugar container," I mentioned.

"Well, that one's not here and," she said as she tore open the red one, "they're not holding sugar." She took out a capsule and showed it to me.

"It sort of looks like my extra strength Tylenol," I said.

"Foxy," she responded.

I think Sally had called me that once with a wink. It was of course meant to be a joke. But I blushed a little then. And without a doubt I blushed now when Ruth Catherine apparently addressed me with that term. I blushed a lot. "I beg your pardon?"

"Let's see if we can find Mrs. Donohue. How do we get to the basement?"

"This way." I led her there. The only other time I had been in the Magill basement was when we had been given those folding shovels last Sunday morning. It seemed like a hundred years ago. Like the rest of the house this morning, the basement was empty. "What did you mean . . ."

"Shhh." Ruth Catherine put a finger to my lips. I liked the feeling. "Can you hear that?"

I listened intensely. Sure enough, I could hear a very soft voice talking. No, wait. There were two voices. Was the second one singing? It was impossible to make out what was being said (or sung).

"It's coming from over here." I followed Ruth Catherine to a side wall. There was an opening. It was a well hidden door that was now slightly ajar. The voices came from behind that door. Ruth Catherine drew a gun from a hidden holster and slowly began to open the door wider. I cringed when the door creaked, but luckily the voices continued as before. The small room we entered was of course empty, but there was a stone staircase leading down at one end. We slowly descended the steps, Ruth Catherine with gun held in front of her in the forward position.

And then I saw Mrs. Donohue snapping pictures with her phone and talking at the same time. Not to the other person sitting on the nearby chair whose back was facing us. "Did you get that?" she asked. "Yea, it's clearer than the other one. Keep going," a man's voice with an odd accent answered her obviously on speakerphone. Mrs. Donohue was photographing Sophie's notebook page by page. Her tote bag was lying on the floor. Was that Sophie in the chair? It was hard for me to tell for sure until the singing started again. That was Sophie's slightly off-key voice. I've never heard anything so beautiful.

> "I know a dark, secluded place,
> A place where no one knows your face,
> A glass of wine, a fast embrace,
> It's called Hernando's Hideaway . . ."

Before Sophie could sing the climactic "Olé," my damned cell phone rang. Mrs. Donohue looked up, heard the Fifth Brandenburg, saw us, raised her gun, (Did everyone in this town carry a gun?) shot twice at us, then ran in the opposite direction from where we were.

I looked at Ruth Catherine who, like me, had crouched down when the gun had been raised at us. "Sorry," I said.

We ran down the remaining stone stairs. "Sophie, how are you?"

"Feeling no pain, boss, just a little woozy. I think she gave me something, put something in her famous tot hoddy."

"I'm going after her," Ruth Catherine said, "you two stay here."

"Not on your life," Sophie stood up with a little difficulty. "We wouldn't miss this for the world."

Before Ruth Catherine could put her foot down, I said with what I hoped was my most beguiling manner, "Please, special agent, special practitioner of modern medicine and biofeedback, special lady. We'll be careful."

With a huge sigh, she relented. "All right, you can follow me, but please stay back a sensible distance."

"Thanks, toots," Sophie giggled and we were off down what looked like an underground passageway built out of stone, ancient stone. We proceeded under the length of the house and then under the front lawn of the Magill property. I could tell that because periodically there were glass covered openings in the ceiling which both let in light and showed us what was above us. "Harry," Sophie was not too drugged out to make this deduction, "I bet dollars to doughnuts that every time I thought I felt some invisible person looking at me, it was some ratfink peering up at me through one of these damned transoms! So maybe I'm not crazy after all."

"Maybe not, my dear Sophie."

The passageway had been heading downwards for a bit and now straightened out. "Now we seem to be under the beach," I remarked. As I said this, we heard several gunshots quite a distance ahead of us. "Oh no, what next?" We increased our pace and soon could see daylight ahead of us. And Ruth Catherine. Or rather the body of Ruth Catherine on the ground stretched back against a wall. "Oh God, is she dead?"

"No, you can't get rid of me that easily, Harry. It's just a minor flesh wound in my arm" That smile again. This was indeed Wonder Woman, without any question.

"Let's see if I can help you with that." I couldn't believe it. Sophie had carried her treasure-filled tote bag during this entire underground trek from which she had just retrieved some pertinent medical supplies.

"That Donohue woman must have arranged to be picked up at noon, four minutes ago. I saw her get into a small boat when I got to the entrance of the cave. That's when she shot me, and I scooted back in here. I called the agency for help, but they said the Coast Guard will take some time to get to the yacht. I'm afraid they're all going to get away. Do you know someone else with a power boat?"

Sophie said, "I'll call Billy Lee Baxter to see if he can pick us up. Where are we?"

"We're at the entrance to the largest cave in the cliffs. It's a recognizable landmark."

As Sophie made her call, I said, "I feel like an idiot saying this, but what the hell are you two talking about? I don't have the least idea."

"Walk a bit forward and see where we are, Harry."

I followed Ruth Catherine's directive and exited the stone passageway. I could see now that the passageway led from the basement of the Magill house all the way to this spot, the mouth of the large cave that Tom had taken us past on that ill-fated sunset cruise six days ago. The darkness of the cave prevented the passageway from being seen. There was a slip of shoreline in front of me at which a boat could land. Ruth Catherine now with a professional looking bandaged arm and Nurse Sophie Nightingale joined me. It was raining quite a bit. Unbelievably, Sophie pulled out two pocket umbrellas for Ruth Catherine's and my use. She pulled up the hood of her own sweatshirt.

"Now we know how the drug smugglers operate," Ruth Catherine told us. "Hallucinogenic drugs, especially the new and dangerous ones called Foxy or Foxy Methoxy are smuggled into Havenport hidden inside those harmless looking cat clocks which must be ferried somehow from the yacht by smaller boats to this cave. They are then carried underground through that stone corridor to the Magill house from which the drugs are distributed to dealers."

"I had read that pirates used to operate in these waters in the 18th century. I bet they built that passageway to sneak their booty into the village literally under the feet of the authorities," said Sophie.

Ruth Catherine went on: "Very interesting, Sophie. Henry Greenstone must have found out about this smuggling route and used it to his advantage. It must have been easy for him when he rented the Magill house and difficult when Madge moved in. You can see how helpful it was for him to have the housekeeper on his payroll. And, I guess, the local constable, her son."

Before we could talk about this further, a boat whistle told us that Billy Lee Baxter had arrived in the Nora B. "Here is the location of the yacht the Jade Pebble," Ruth Catherine handed her phone to Billy Lee. "The Coast Guard just texted it to me. That's where Mrs. Donohue and the pilot of her little motorboat are headed, I'm sure. I'd like to overtake her before she reaches the yacht. It's anchored in international waters."

"I'll do my best. Miss Xerxes told me this will help catch the bums who blew up the Sea Witch and the Bensons. I'll do more than my freakin' best." I liked Billy Lee just as I had liked Tom Wright.

We were moving at quite a clip. I was white-knuckling the side of the boat pretty tightly. I was sitting quite stiffly and didn't say much. But I was on the boat. And I wasn't panicking. It was too important. We had to apprehend those responsible for all the deaths, all the grief. We had to find Sally. I believed all would be revealed if we only could catch up with the boat propelling Mrs. Donohue to the yacht and, I assumed, freedom. I had worked with great actors in my day, but both Edna Donohue and her son were definitely their equals. It had never occurred to me that they were playing roles, lying through their teeth every moment. How did they do it, and, importantly, why did they do it? I wouldn't rest until I found out. That was one reason why I somehow was able to block my fears and stay on this very bumpy boat ride. I was also doing some biofeedback technique as well. I think it was working even without the equipment.

"Thar she be!" Billy Lee shouted. And indeed the little motor boat with its two occupants could be seen in the distance ahead of us. It was apparent that we were able to move through the waves at a much faster speed than they.

"Of course," as Sophie rationally said to me raising her voice to be heard over the wind, "if we can see them, they can see us."

And she was right. They did see us and they turned around and headed straight for us. Ruth Catherine raised her gun. They got closer and closer. We could make out some physical details of the people. I could see Mrs. Donohue's paisley head scarf and black raincoat. I could make out what the boat's pilot was wearing. "Oh, my God, not again," Sophie cried out. And through the wind and the rain I saw what she saw. The pilot was dressed exactly as the laughing rifleman had dressed on the cliff. And then he raised himself up and we saw that he was carrying a rifle. And I saw ("O gods and goddesses!") the pilot of the boat and the killer of Tom Wright was Sally.

And Sally was firing that rifle at us. And she hit Billy Lee, which in a moment caused our boat to spin around. And she hit the gas tank, which in a moment caused the Nora B to explode.

Epilogue

THE CAMERA PEOPLE WERE ALTERING their positions. Stagehands were scurrying around moving set pieces and teleprompters. Lights were being refocused. The musical director was receiving information from someone talking in his earphone. The Tony Awards broadcast was live and so all these adjustments had to be made during the (many) commercial breaks. A young man with earphones on asked us to move to the predetermined aisle seats. A woman with a handheld camera was already in the aisle now a foot away from me. She smiled halfheartedly.

The ceremony was thankfully almost over. It was running late. People were nervous. People were tense. I was neither. Even though the final category for which I was nominated was coming up next (Best Play of the Year) and even though our play's three other nominations (Best Actor, Best Supporting Actor, and, gasp! Best Director) had been won by others, I was not nervous. I was not tense. You see I was alive. And that was more important than winning Best Play of the Year.

I closed my eyes and relished being alive. I never imagined I would be. When the boat exploded, I was hurled into the churning waves by the fireball. I was burned but still alive. My lifejacket was still on but, when I finally located Sophie in the maelstrom, hers was not. Somehow I managed to hold on to her unconscious body. Somehow I managed to avoid the rifle fire aimed at us when it wasn't aimed at Ruth Catherine who was holding up the unconscious Billy Lee Baxter. How long did this continue? Centuries? Millennia? I'm not sure. But it did eventually end when the Coast Guard saved us and captured Thelma Donohue and Louise Wright.

The back story details of how Mrs. Donohue and the Bensons had been corrupted by oodles of money (and clocks I suppose) into assisting the drug smugglers didn't really interest me. The details of how Robby had been seduced by his lifelong obsession for Sally and his lifelong hatred of Edward and his Yale-boy entitlements into throwing away his career, his sense of self-respect and honor didn't really interest me all that much.

Sally's pathological need for power was a slightly more interesting story. I'm thinking of including it in my new play. Working for the drug dealers as soon as she learned about them, Sally convinced her father to use his fishing boats to ferry the drugs from the yacht eventually to the cave. He did this on six separate occasions but told her he would not participate in this illegal activity any more, beginning with the current caper planned for Thursday night, during the Laurence Little Players' performance. The whole village always attended their shows, so this was always a good time to ensure no witnesses to the smuggling operation.

The smugglers were afraid that Tom would squeal to the police or to me when I arrived. They were afraid of his evening talks with me (the eminent amateur sleuth) and especially his sunset cruise with Sophie and me. This would be the perfect time to kill him off. It was left to the evil mastermind Sally to work out the details of the murder.

She came up with a pip. She and Robby were both on the cliffs in different places. In the unlikely chance that she would miss, he would have a second chance. But she didn't miss. Throughout their childhood, Sally and Robby practiced marksmanship in the summers with Edward and eventually became as good a shot as he.

Speaking of Edward, Sally also devised the way of getting Madge to sell the house to the drug traffickers. Intense grief from the loss of her son would compel her to cut all ties with Havenport. The loss would be either from his supposed suicide or, should he survive the fall, from state execution. Even though she had been both Henry Greenstone's and Robby's mistress for years, (He and the other people on the yacht were of course all arrested by the Coast Guard), she pretended to be in love with Edward. On that infamous Saturday night, she got Edward to take her to the backroom of The Copper Moon. They looked happy in that photograph, but there was a mickey in his champagne which caused him to pass out. When he woke later that night in his car near the general store, he thought he had dreamed what Sally had told him she was going to do, but he discovered it was true. He read her text messages telling him that she had used his rifle to kill her father because he was going to send her away from Edward, to part the two of them forever. She told him to bury all his weapons so that he would not be implicated and then meet her at the airport so that they could fly off to a foreign clime and be together forever. When he heard me call out his name on the beach, he saw Jessie Gillespie bash me on the head with a bat, (That was one of the things I later recalled through biofeedback and of which I am more that rightly humiliated.) and then he was also hit from behind by Robby. He was dropped into Noah Benson's limo and driven directly to the airport VIP lounge. Nora's story that he had first come to their house had been fabricated to alter the timeline. Edward's bicycle was later brought to the Benson house by Robby.

Edward was then given two Foxy capsules in the VIP lounge and in a hallucinogenic state made to believe that he saw Sally jump off the observation deck due to patricidal guilt. Dressed as cleaning women, Sally and Mrs. Donohue had sat in the VIP lounge with Edward playing with his altered mind. When Noah Benson saw in his hidden spot at the airport that Sophie and I had arrived, he made a call, and the final segment of this bizarre Hitchcock-worthy plot was put into motion. Mrs. Gillespie tied herself up in the back of the airport Cousin Carrie's. (I understand old Jessie and other key players of Cousin Carrie's are all in the hoosegow as well.) Edward's cell phone was taken from him to be put later in my jacket pocket by Mrs. Donohue. All records of his text messages to Sally had been deleted. Edward was given a third Foxy and convinced that he wanted to join his beloved in the afterlife. It was also Mrs. Donohue, the brilliant actress that she was, who in her Tony-deserving performance as the older cleaning woman told me where to find Edward.

Speaking of the Tonys, the commercial was over and the final two awards were to be given out: first, Best Play and then, finally, Best Musical. I may disagree with their order of importance. However, I shall be the good sport that I am and pretend that the outcome of my final category matters tremendously to me. When, actually, the reception of the memorial to Tom that Thursday night several weeks ago was of much greater import to me. In four words: it was a triumph. The kiss on the cheek and the pat on the hand I received from the openly weeping Miss Laurence meant everything to me.

Time is fleeting now, so I shall add only two more sad facts. Sally had faked her death so that she could later freely run off to South America for more fun and games with the drug cartel. She didn't seem to care a bit that poor Roxanne Willis from the movie theatre had been selected to be Sally's body double, so to speak.

They're announcing the nominees now. So if you want to learn the details of the incredibly complex code on the restaurant review posters, you'd better ask Sophie. She's still in the hospital recovering from her severe burns, but they say she'll be fine. I never understood the minutia that she (and not the Federal code-breakers) worked out but the three colors were assigned to three groups of locals performing different tasks in the smuggling operation. The altered numbers in the dates told then how many words down in the review they were to count to find the first word of their message and then count accordingly to proceed to the next word and so forth. Each group's message told them the place they were to assemble and the time to do so. I think one message read: eight (o'clock) kelp. The second was eight thirty cave. You get the idea. Oh by the way, when Robby heard we had become entangled in the kelp forest, he almost had a conniption for that was the spot in which Noah Benson always transferred the boxes of clocks which he picked up from the yacht a few days before the actual big night. Sophie's success in breaking the code allowed the cops to apprehend the remaining groups of locals in the act of transferring the drugs.

Speaking of Noah Benson, he and his wife had been foolish enough to argue with Sally over their cut of the profits when they visited the Jade Pebble. Not a smart move. You've heard of *The Big Bang Theory*?

Oh, they just read off my name as one of the nominees. I smiled warmly to Ms. Camera Lady in the aisle. Oh, they're opening the envelope.

I hope Sophie and Billy Lee and Ruth Catherine are watching this moment from the hospital and Edward and Madge and Barbara. I'm worried again about Barbara. How will she cope now knowing her daughter murdered her own father? However, the others are all doing well. Even Edward. It really is a miracle. Tomorrow I shall return to Havenport to see how Sophie is doing and say goodbye for a while to Ruth Catherine. As soon as she has fully recovered, she will be assigned to a new case in another town. I hope we can keep in touch. I want very much to keep in touch. Luckily her brother-in-law will not be going with her wherever she goes, but St. Roscoe will.

Speaking of the dentist, I finally found out what Tom's cryptic message to me meant. It was intended to direct me to his killer.

"Aches . . . Tooth . . . Aches . . . Tooth . . . Tooths . . . Aches . . . ." did not refer to a dentist. It referred to Sally.

You see, when I was recuperating before traveling to New York for the Tonys, I looked over Tom's paperback copy of *King Lear* to help pass the time. Tom had marked pertinent passages with relevant annotations.

When I got to the fourth scene of Act I, it was impossible to miss that he had written in red ink the name "Sally" next to this line:

"How sharper than a serpent's tooth it is to have a thankless child."

With his last breath in the motor boat he had thought of this line and had wanted to say "Serpent's tooth." But he had then such difficulty pronouncing plosives, he tried to get out: "snake's tooth" rather than serpent's. I heard it wrongly as "aches tooth."

"How sharper than a serpent's tooth it is to have a thankless child." Indeed. That Shakespeare was a genius. Speaking of geniuses:

"And the Tony award for Best Play goes to: *The Readiness Is All* written by Harrison Hunt."

I turned to my father and laughed. He laughed too and hugged me. Yes, I took my father to the Tony's. After my head injury on the rocks when I was a child, I must have experienced a memory loss. I had forgotten an incident, an important incident, as important as my rescue from the rocks by the Coast Guard. It was my father's visit to my hospital room. His legs had been badly damaged trying to recover the oars and he was in terrible pain walking to the side of my bed clumping along on his metal crutches. He held my hand and sobbed. As Madge had done in Edward's hospital room.

And I had forgotten this sweet, loving moment from my childhood. Until biofeedback brought it back to me. Our relationship had been very strained all these years. "How sharper than a serpent's tooth it is to have a thankless child."

But now it will be better. As I walked up the stairs to Radio City Music Hall's gigantic stage to collect my award, I must confess that winning it did in fact matter a little to me, maybe more than a little. Of course I was grateful to be alive. But there are other things to be grateful for as well, aren't there? I'm grateful that Sophie is still in my life. I'm grateful I shall now be taking my father to the famed Tony winners' dinner celebration tonight. I've always wanted to go there. I hear it's THE event of the year. Everyone will be there. I'm grateful that in a couple of weeks Sophie and I will be in London preparing the West End transfer of *The Readiness Is All*. I understand ticket sales are buzzing already over there. And now with my Tony win and all the hoopla surrounding my solving the Havenport murders, well, it's destined to be a triumph.

Made in the USA
Middletown, DE
18 February 2017